ANYWHERE

A LONG LAKES THRILLER

ANTONELLA RIVALTA

ISBN: 979-8-9861752-2-5

Cover design by: Art Painter

Library of Congress Control Number: 2018675309

Printed in the United States of America

PROLOGUE

To anyone passing by Room 17 in the ICU of Knoxville Hospital, it looked like a grieving wife was mourning the loss of her dearest husband.

But that was not what this was.

The realization hit the man more forcefully than ever as he slowly came out of the fog his brain had been in for the past two months.

He kept his eyes closed as Jessica, his loving wife, leaned in, her breath tickling his ear, and quietly described her scheme in detail.

"My dear, although you will never be able to respond to me, I will make my plan clear to you. I have put up with your selfish, narcissistic behavior for long enough. You bought me with a false promise of happiness and limitless wealth, but you lied to me, my husband. Too many lies, and too much misery. And so I have put an end to it. I will take my life back, love and be loved by the man who is helping me lock you up in your malfunctioning body. To put it in your language, your hard drive is infected with a powerful virus and it's going to crash."

When Doctor Randall Sparks came into the room Jessica stopped talking long enough to step away, and he cracked an eye just long enough to see her greet her lover with a kiss. Their conversation went immediately to the plans they had made for the evening, dinner and dancing on a riverboat as it steamed along the Tennessee River. Jessica made a mockery of apologizing to the man who was essentially dead to her, emotionally and very soon, physically. The night would be a celebration of their success, of being rid of a man she hated enough to commit murder.

The first thing the patient needed to do was to hack into the monitors beside his bed. His laptop was on the nightstand, still charging after all this time. It was a stroke of luck that Jessica had left it there, and now he set to work to derail the program that monitored his vital signs. He recalled an article he had read detailing this new threat to hospital security and he easily completed the task.

There would be one last check from the nurse before the shift change. From there, the staff would leave him alone if the monitors didn't betray him. His plan would need to get him back in

this bed by midnight, the usual time for a mid-shift bed check. Ever since the drugs had begun to wear off and sensible thoughts filled his formerly numb mind, exercise had been a daily thing. It wasn't difficult to maintain strength within the four walls of his room, and the added benefit of physical therapy only augmented rebuilding his strength.

His clothes were still in the small closet, hanging for two months as though in anticipation of this night. He dressed quickly, surprised as he realized he'd obviously lost weight. Undaunted by that it was a matter of a few minutes to find his way to the elevator that would take him to the lobby.

The lone assassin was able to hail a cab and paid for it with the cash sewn into a secret pocket in the jacket lining. He was always prepared, and not even his wife knew of the myriad of ways in which he assured himself of victories over any circumstance. The ride from East Knoxville took South Central Street down to the dock where the *Dixie Lady* riverboat was receiving the evening's passengers.

He paid the cabbie and scanned the area for a way onboard. The dinner cruise would have been pre-booked, so getting inside presented a problem. Even though it was dark, the lights along the dock area in addition to the well-lit riverboat served to provide substantial illumination for the evening. Passengers boarding the paddlewheel boat were cheerful, anticipating a good time in a unique environment.

The patient, now a spurned husband, needed a way onto the riverboat. As he watched the scene, a crewmember dressed in dark trousers and a white shirt caught his attention. That man was able to board the boat without any interference. Taking off his own jacket and the sapphire colored silk tie, the betrayed husband simply draped it over the handle of a dolly already loaded with three boxes of Jack Daniels whiskey. A rag that had been tossed aside was placed over the jacket, and he was easily waved aboard and directed to the bar as he wheeled all of it up the ramp. He delivered it, keeping his head down to avoid eye contact with anyone. What was needed now was a way to become a part of this crowd by reassuming the image of a sophisticated and well-dressed man. Even though the suit fit more loosely than before he had been confined to a hospital bed, the cut of it was so well defined that to most people it was imperceptible. Now it was a waiting game.

The boat's interior was lavishly furnished, a throwback to the heyday of river travel aboard the elegant Southern riverboats. The walls were covered in brocade wallpaper in a hue reminiscent of port wine. Embellished gilded frames and crown molding ran all throughout the boat's great rooms. There were three dining rooms, one on each of the three decks, with capacity for one hundred people. It appeared that most of the passengers were couples, probably looking for a romantic evening on the waters of the great Tennessee River. This riverboat was one of several that traveled the waterway, and although not original, it was a beautiful recreation of a bygone era. Wearied from the effort, the recently comatose man took it all in and imagined exacting his revenge. He repeated to himself, '*vengeance is mine, saith the LORD*'. Indeed, he counted himself lord of his own life, and perfectly able to collect his vengeance on those who betrayed him.

From a vantage point camouflaged by a grouping of Majestic Palms, he waited for Jessica and Dr. Randall Sparks to board. From his position he could see everyone as they came through the main entrance. At exactly eight o'clock, the willowy blonde appeared on the arm of a dull-looking man. So, his beautiful wife was wooing an inconsequential man into committing murder. He wondered what else she had planned for him.

The couple were directed to a dining room at the forward section of the boat's second deck. He followed them at a distance, creating a plan as he did so. It wouldn't do for him to be noticed by anyone as being connected to them, so he ducked into the galley once they were seated. It wasn't difficult to find a waiter's jacket, a plausible disguise considering the impromptu nature of this entire evening. He avoided being called upon to serve, and instead spent the next hour waiting for the opportunity to carry out the plan that had finally crystalized for him.

The beauty of a riverboat is its elegance, and the intimacy. Cruise ships are too big, too exuberant. There is a romance on a riverboat to which one can succumb with ease, a relief from what has been left on the riverbank. The assassin was sensing that now, and the relief he would feel at saving the woman he had once loved from doing the unthinkable.

Drinking to excess always begins with just one, and several complimentary drinks were delivered to Jessica's table. When the waiter was asked who sent them, he merely replied 'an admirer'. The man knew Jessica would be flattered by this, and not question it twice.

When Jessica and her doctor finally decided to get some fresh air out on the deck, the man was close behind them. They were both tipsy thanks to the several drinks they had accepted, and there was a noticeable wobble as they walked along the railing, remarking on the beautiful night sky. The time was now, and while they pointed to the stars, he ran towards them and knocked into them with so much force that they immediately crashed through the spindle-shaped railing and into the churning waters created by the giant paddle wheel.

The same one who would claim credit for their deaths nearly went overboard with them but managed to grab hold of a part of the railing that supported his weight. He scrambled to climb back onto the deck, grateful that those pounds he had lost were perhaps the difference between plunging into the frigid water below and being able to hang onto the railing. He needed to get back inside. It wouldn't do for him to be at the scene of the accident, as it would later be described. Too much alcohol would be blamed for the unfortunate tragedy.

A man with such a deadly mission must be clever, he needed to hide in plain sight until the riverboat docked. The faux server continued to roam the dining rooms, always looking occupied until finally the cruise ended back at the beginning. It was then that something like fear stabbed at the killer's heart as he made his way down the gang plank and hailed a cab back to the hospital.

When the night nurse came into Room 17 on her evening rounds she found the patient tucked into his bed, just where she had left him.

CHAPTER 1

Doris let out a yelp of delight as she entered another world within the virtual reality apparatus she was wearing. To say it was fun was an understatement. She had lost all concept of the world outside of what she was experiencing now, nothing else existed.

The device had been loaned to her by a new friend, and the thought of him brought on a different sort of reality. Doris experienced a sudden pang of guilt and shame to be enjoying herself so thoroughly as her husband of thirty years lay in a hospital bed, a victim of a devastating stroke. Brent had been bedridden in a pricey, long-term convalescent hospital for two years, and that meant two years of agonizing loneliness for the still vibrant and pretty woman.

Thankfully, Brent was a man who believed in and practiced planning for the future. He had wisely invested in an insurance policy that was now bearing the brunt of the cost of the Chattanooga facility, giving Doris a measure of independence from what might have been an unbearable burden. As it was, she was able to keep her beloved home in Long Lakes, the one that she and Brent had built, a home meant for what they believed would be *happily ever after.*

One of the things that Doris and Brent had enjoyed was collecting art. The house was filled with the pieces they had collected while traveling the world. Brent discovered a love of carvings and statues, both new and old. Doris made sure to keep them on display after he was hospitalized, despite her lack of the same appreciation. Her favorites were the paintings that lined the walls of their house. It was the memories that were triggered by the art, the joy that had accompanied each discovery.

Doris carried a measure of guilt for having sought out companionship as Brent measured his days with an irreversible condition. She missed nights out on the arm of a man, the dancing and movies and... Brent was truly the love of her life.

It was a long list of activities she would never again share with her husband. Doris needed to be with someone because being alone and the emptiness of solitude were not something she handled well. When she decided to try out a dating site, simply to find someone companionable and fun, she was surprised and a little afraid of the man who eventually helped to restore her

love of life; she was able to forget for just brief moments that Brent wasn't the man making it possible.

Doris had been honest in her desire for companionship only, making the situation regarding Brent's condition very clear. She wasn't looking for marriage, only a reprieve from loneliness. She wouldn't be faulted or scorned for seeking out friendship. There had been several 'matches' based on the information she shared, but none of them had seemed right for her. She dated a few of them, then politely declined any additional engagements with them. She saw a couple of the men take a keen interest in her beautiful home, as though they might have designs on it. Doris wasn't anyone's fool, and she didn't need a roommate. She wanted a friendly escort to the places she couldn't face going to alone.

Then, almost miraculously, the right man did respond. Mark was good-looking, with an impressive head of salt and pepper hair that topped off a well-kept physique. He was charming and, in Doris's estimation, honest. He treated her with respect and a degree of empathy when she, on occasion, shared her loneliness after losing her life with Brent. Mark was himself a widower but had taken his grief at losing his wife as a catalyst for living his life as though she would have approved. His conscience was not assaulted by how he was doing it.

Mark Matheson had given Doris the virtual reality headset she was now enjoying. He owned a business that produced these little wonders, and that made the man even more interesting and, when she dared to admit it, desirable. It was almost too wonderful to be in the company of a man she found so congenial and happy. She sometimes imagined sharing her life with Mark, wondering what it would be like to find herself available. Those thoughts were met with a type of self-loathing, an accusation that she didn't have the right to move her husband out of the way of selfish hopes of contentment.

Mark often took her dancing and proved to be a marvelous partner on the dance floor. His choice of restaurants always pleased her own palette, and his love of old movies provided many nights of casual intimacy. Doris found herself falling in love for the second time in her life, but with the knowledge that marriage was not an option for her. She let Mark into her world, into a life that she admitted had been so lonely and empty for the last two years. Was it possible that she could love two men at the same time?

Doris was aboard a rollercoaster, experiencing the thrills of going up and then plunging down as the track carried her on an undulating thrill ride. Mark was right, the technology that could produce such a marvel made Doris even more appreciative of this man who had become almost like an addiction. The more time she spent with him, the harder it had become to imagine a life without him.

At the moment the rollercoaster ride was making Doris laugh out loud and shriek with delight at the twists and turns. The headset hugged her ears, making it impossible to hear the back door open or the approach of footsteps on her hardwood floors. She was enjoying the ride and reflecting on the genius of this thing called virtual reality. Seated as she was in her living room, the figure in black thought it was a peculiar sight to watch the woman as she experienced the illusion in which she was trapped. Her perception of reality was isolated within the headset, making her a prisoner to its power to block out the world around her.

The intruder approached Doris. She remained completely unaware, and as the individual walked around her to face her, it was obvious that she could not see or sense anyone else. The sounds of the 'game' leaked out into the room, its volume cranked up to a maximum level. Doris had no idea that the rollercoaster was about to morph into a vehicle of death, a danger she now faced without aware-ness. The madman before her smiled at what was about to happen.

It was quick, a sudden move that sent Doris reeling back-wards. She reached for the headset to relieve the lurching in her stomach from what she thought was the game's rollercoaster, only to feel the violent impact as her head hit the floor. Doris quickly faded into unconsciousness, but not enough to satisfy the betrayal and madness that propelled the assassin.

The woman was not dead, and so the mission was incomplete. The headset was yanked from Doris's head, and in one final act of violence, the force of impact from a carved stone statue cracked her skull and ended her life.

As blood poured from her skull, Doris might have had one last moment of recognition when she breathed her last breath with regret and sorrow.

CHAPTER 2

John Watson was spending the evening the best way he knew how—with a favorite book, a glass of sherry and his dutiful and faithful companion, Sherlock. The feline was perched on the arm of John's weathered leather chair, appearing to read along with him.

"Sherlock, my man, tonight we are adventuring with Athos, Porthos and Aramis, and of course the gallant D'Artagnan. I believe that you, Monsieur Sherlock, would have been a Musketeer par excellence."

The response from the black Maine Coon was a renewed purring sound that reverberated on the ancient leather, warming John's heart for the affection he knew it represented. In the Long Lakes community in south central

Tennessee, the traditional rite of passage included the acquisition of new friends to share in this idyllic spot. Since moving here after retiring from his medical practice following the passing of his beloved wife, John had sought out a new life. This one was proving to be a most rich, interesting chapter indeed for the dapper Englishman. There was always something different to experience in this corner of the world, from the Southern cuisine to the Smoky Mountains, to the many different people who'd come here from all over the world. Chief among his new acquaintances was the lovely Michelle Michaels, a woman he now considered a special lady friend. Meeting her had given him a literal new lease on life.

Michelle was unavailable this evening, unfortunately. She was with some of the ladies of Long Lakes, enjoying a game of Mahjong. He was also an aficionado of the game, but wouldn't dream of intruding upon the weekly ladies-only event. No matter. He and Sherlock were old friends, and spending the evening together was a pleasant way to while away the hours.

As John turned the page, his phone buzzed and played the distinctive ring tone, 'Hail Britannia'. His native England was never far from his heart, or memories.

The screen told him that it was Michelle calling, bringing a smile to his face. He wondered what could possibly prompt her to call while engaged in her Mahjong game.

John answered with a cheery hello that was rewarded by hearing Michelle's sweet voice. "Hi, neighbor," she said.

"Hello back," he said, smiling because he could see her smile. "What on earth could tear you away from your game?"

"Oh, we haven't even started yet. Doris is late, and not answering her phone. I'd hate to go all the way there. Could you check on her?"

"Of course, I am delighted to be of service. We shouldn't like your game to be further delayed." Over the past months, John had developed a deep interest in ensuring Michelle's happiness, even if was only a game of Mahjong. "I'll send Doris on her way to you."

John called to Sherlock that he was heading out to see about their neighbor. The elegant black cat was at the door before the man finished his sentence. Bright golden eyes shone up at him as John prepared for their short walk by slipping on Sherlock's blue harness. Donning his old hat, John opened the door, and they stepped out into the twilight. As they walked toward Doris's house, the night overtook them.

Though John Watson was a relatively new resident in the Long Lakes community, he continued to feel the attraction to the setting and the people he had met. Michelle had been a welcome surprise; he'd been certain that he would never find a suitable companion again after his wife's death. At that time, he'd been left a sad and lonely man, consoled only by his faithful Sherlock. Now, nothing was left of that man. These days, he lived a robust and happy life in the hills of Tennessee, perfectly content in his cottage that sat among the trees and lakes that made the gated development such a lovely place to live. Life was as it should be.

John stepped aside as Sherlock made his way through the door and out onto the porch. He stretched, shaking off the lethargy he'd acquired by being indoors for hours. A bird answered the chirping of a cricket as lightning bugs, nature's miniature lanterns, shone the way. It would be the last time, perhaps, before cooler weather prevailed. The sun had set itself resolutely behind a stand of trees with only the hint of a halo framing its descent.

"Let us carry on, my boy. We have been assigned a small task by Michelle. We shan't disappoint her." Sherlock seemed to understand the importance of what his man was saying, a shared sense of responsibility to the task at hand. With his tail straight up, he helped John to set a pace as they headed down the walkway and onto the road for their short journey to Doris's house.

John noticed his new friend Valentina Bianco as she appeared from the direction of her home next door to his, going for her evening walk, he assumed. John admired the pretty woman from Italy, carving out a life for herself in a new country, running a business that seemed to be successful. He knew she was recently divorced and the mother of a college-aged daughter. Those details only added to his sense of appreciation of her.

Valentina shouted a hello and waved back at John as he headed up Doris's walk and onto the porch. "Lovely night for a stroll, isn't it?"

"Yes it is," she said, checking her watch before heading off down the road. Doris's home was unlit. The porch light wasn't even on, which he found strange, especially if she'd gone out, expecting to be home after dark. John rang the doorbell, then knocked loudly. "Doris? It's John, from down the road."

There was no answer.

On a whim, he tried the front door, only to find that it was unlocked. It seemed odd, as unlocked doors were a breach in common sense to the former pediatrician. His penchant for playing detective did make him curious, so he pushed it open slightly.

John entered the house, calling out Doris's name. No response, only a bothersome sense of trouble in the quiet of an empty house. Rather than stumble in the darkness of the unfamiliar home, John pulled out his trusty, small flashlight.

As John turned a corner to head to the kitchen and family room area, arcing the light to and fro, the beam of his light caught on a grisly sight.

Blood. Too much blood.

He froze, his own blood turning to ice.

It was Doris, sprawled on her back on the floor in front of the kitchen island. He shone his flashlight on the walls, searching for a light switch. Locating one, he switched it on, instantly seeing more clearly the awful sight.

The poor, older woman's graying hair was drenched in blood, which spilled in a pool underneath her, puddling on the beautiful Italian tile floors. It looked like a severe blow to her head.

Recalling his training as a physician, John placed his finger on the woman's neck and hoped for a pulse. There was none.

John reached into his coat pocket and retrieved his cell phone, hand trembling so much that he decided to speak to the phone rather than attempt to dial. The dispatcher on the other end of his call to 911 assured him that emergency personnel would be there as quickly as possible. He was instructed to stay put, and to not touch anything.

Sherlock tugged at his harness as John looked around the room. He could see where Doris must have been sitting, taking note of the chair legs. He wondered briefly how she could have fallen backwards with such force, but he was so affected by the tragedy before him that John let his curiosity park itself for the time being. Surely this was the scene of a most unfortunate accident.

As John ruminated on the scene before him, his phone began to ring out 'Hail Britannia'. It was Michelle.

"Oh, my dear, I'm afraid I have dreadful news." John could hear other voices in the background, and he assumed it was her Mahjong companions.

"What is it?" she asked.

"Yes, it's... well, I found Doris.' He paused briefly but the words just lingered on his tongue. Finally, he found his voice. "My dear Michelle, our friend Doris is quite dead. She appears to have had a very bad fall and, well... the ambulance is on the way."

Michelle gasped and attempted to relay this news to Lola and Delta. John heard a shriek, and then a mix of women's voices, frantic. He gathered that the three of them were on their way to Doris's house.

"Yes, well, I suppose that's acceptable. But you cannot come inside, I will meet you in the front yard." With that, the conversation ended, and John imagined the three women scurrying out of the clubhouse, alerting anyone in their path to this most recent news.

John took one last look around the kitchen and living room, pulling at Sherlock's leash to persuade him to follow. Sherlock seemed very interested in the scene, especially Doris's bloodied face. John shooed the cat away from the body, checking his paws to make certain he hadn't

stepped into the blood. The two of them made their way outside to wait for Michelle and the other ladies, and for the ambulance.

As he was sitting on the front porch with Sherlock in his arms, John saw Valentina once again as she passed beneath a streetlamp, returning from her short walk. He motioned her up wildly, and Valentina approached.

As she reached the edge of Doris's lot, two headlights cut their way up the street, coming to an abrupt stop in front of the neighboring property. John realized it was Lola's car. When it stopped, the doors flew open as Michelle, Delta and Lola all seemed to be forcefully ejected from the vehicle.

"Oh, John! What on earth happened?" Michelle asked, her face white.

"My dear, it is a grim scene. I find it hard to imagine how it happened, but there seems to be nothing to suggest violence or, well... murder."

Michelle shuddered visibly and looked over at Valentina.

"John, Michelle. What happened? Is Doris...?"

John shook his head.

"She's dead? How? I mean, is there any clue as to how it happened?"

John sighed. "No, my dear, I didn't see a clue to anything save for a very bad fall. It is so very unfortunate." It was very mysterious to him.

In the dark of night with only the light of the amber-colored streetlamp, the five people stood on the front lawn of their friend's house. A strong gust of wind swept in, as though to punctuate the situation. All of them stood facing each other, questions etched on their faces as the absoluteness of the situation began to sink in.

Doris was dead.

The wail of an ambulance split the night sky, lights flashing a menacing message to all who could hear or see its approach. As it parked in the driveway, the emergency medical team rushed into action, gathering their gear and the gurney on which Doris's body would be conveyed. A firetruck pulled up to the curb, as well as a police car. There would be no lack of curiosity or conversation in the morning. The tranquility of Long Lakes was now entirely displaced in the wake of this latest tragedy.

John was pulled aside by a police officer, Officer O'Mara, to give his account of events. He was able to give a detailed version of his entry into the house, the light switch and then his discovery of Doris on the floor.

Sherlock stayed close to John, but the cat observed everything. John remembered his curiosity with Doris's head and face and wondered if he should mention it to Officer O'Mara, but in the end decided it wasn't important.

The women had all gathered on the walkway leading up to the front porch. Their questions came out like a hail of bullets, and in deference to their friendships with Doris, John answered as best he could. In truth, he had little information to offer, only his discovery and subsequent call to the 911 operator.

There were a few neighbors beginning to migrate to Doris's house. The sight and sound of the emergency vehicles descending on the property had led even the less curious of the neighbors to investigate. After about a half-hour, John wished to avoid being questioned by anyone else, and so he suggested to Michelle and her friends that it would be better to take their leave. Michelle and Valentina exchanged looks that said *we'll discuss this later* and agreed with John that the police should be allowed to do their work unhindered by their presence. Lola reluctantly agreed, although it was with the anticipation of alerting the other residents of Long Lakes to this grisly bit of gossip.

As John took Michelle's hand to guide her home, he noticed a slight tremor. The night air was pleasant, the sounds of late autumn lending a bit of comfort. Above all, John intended to protect Michelle as best as he was able. While they walked in silence, it was impossible for him to not speculate on the scene he had witnessed.

The more he thought about it, the more he began to wonder if Doris's death was not an accident.

CHAPTER 3

Valentina woke up early the day after the discovery of her neighbor's death. She hadn't known Doris very well, but she was a pleasant woman, attractive and vibrant. She'd been living alone, due to her husband's unfortunate health issues, which required him to be in a long-term care facility.

The morning fog was typical for this time of the year. Cool air was coming in and settling over the still warm earth, and the foggy veneer would lift to reveal the changing colors that signaled another season had arrived. Valentina loved autumn and the colors that spoke of the warmth of a fire, of soups on the stove; but something was missing...

She missed Jack.

Jack Erikson had entered her life at a time when she thought she could live without love, proving her wrong and bringing with him the care and comfort of companionship and, if she were honest with herself, love. Living in Long Lakes had been a pleasant time for Valentina. Despite the divorce that had rocked her foundation of trust, she had a very dear friend in Michelle, and the new relationship with Jack that had the potential to be lasting.

There had been a couple of bumps in the road. Her meeting with Jack had been entangled with a murder. In an investigation that took Jack out of his normal FBI duties as a fraud investigator, he'd become embroiled in a situation that put both him and Valentina in danger. Warren Harvey, formerly the chief mover-and-shaker in the community, had led them all on a path that involved murder, drugs, and even kidnapping. It had shaken Long Lakes down to its foundation. Even now, months later, Valentina shuddered at the memory of it.

She looked up at the chirping sounds from a tree limb to find it full of blue jays. Past that, the mirror-calm lake. She couldn't look at that lake anymore without thinking of the time she met the actor Wyatt Rogers while kayaking near the home he was leasing. That had been the beginning of another bizarre entanglement with deceit and murder. Thankfully, the guilty had been caught, and in the midst of it, the relationship between two people had found its beginning. Her friend Michelle was bubbling over now with her own affection for John Watson, the kind Englishman who lived next door.

Despite its idyllic setting, there was no shortage of drama around Long Lakes. The thought of Jack brought a smile to her face and a wistful sigh as she sipped her morning coffee. The FBI agent was due back today, and Valentina intended to make his homecoming something special.

As she savored her coffee, Valentina watched the fog suddenly surrender to the first rays of the sun. It was going to be a beautiful day, and hopefully a memorable evening. Her to-do list was long, but by the time Jack arrived for dinner, the house would be decorated with the hues of the season and her kitchen filled with the aromas of butternut squash soup and freshly baked cheese bread. The second course would be (according to Michelle, since it was her recipe), *a good old-fashioned pot roast with root vegetables and soul-satisfying beef gravy that could make a man's heart sing.*

Valentina's heart felt like singing as she thought about being with Jack again. She let the last sip of her coffee warm her throat and her intentions. The fog was completely gone and looking out into the new day she could see the colors of fall in the trees beyond. Leaves showed signs of yellow and orange, even the occasional red; it all made her anticipate the meal preparation and the man for whom she was doing it. Valentina wasn't a woman who depended on a man to complete her, but she was someone who appreciated the enrichment that sharing one's life could bring.

This evening's meal would be a celebration of the new season. She only hoped she could make it as well as Michelle did. Her heart warmed once more, this time with the thought of her friend and the Englishman, John Watson. It wasn't an impossibility to find love and companionship later in life—those two were living proof. The advantage of being comfortable with someone again after losing a first love was part of what they were sharing. Valentina sighed with contentment before her heart felt the twinge of separation as her thoughts turned back to Jack.

The kitchen was ready for action. Valentina was an organized woman and her placement of utensils and the various pots and pans all made sense. Her big farmhouse sink was the center point of the outward-facing wall, with a view of more open space. The symmetry of the space featured plenty of counter tops, and the big six-burner Vulcan stove was the pride of the kitchen.

Valentina felt great contentment here, and she knew that the addition of love would make for a great meal.

Thoughts of the previous evening rambled through her mind as she took the slow cooker from beneath the counter. It only occurred to her as she was setting it up that she hadn't defrosted the roast. Michelle had recommended freezing it, but with everything that had happened the previous night, removing it had been overlooked completely. Sighing, she went to the fridge and took out the hunk of meat. It was solid as a rock.

With a groan and a quick inventory of recipes to replace the roast, Valentina removed her phone from the charger and dialed her friend.

Michelle answered on the third ring as she saw the name of the caller.

"Good morning, Valentina." Michelle's Southern drawl always made Valentina smile, it was a slow and measured way of greeting the world.

"Oh, *buongiorno*. You sound so sweet and happy, that makes me feel better already." "Oh dear, does that mean there's something for me to worry about?"

"No, no…" Valentina chuckled at herself for that moment of panic.

"Not at all. But I forgot to take the roast out of the freezer. Will I need to try and defrost it?" Michelle was quick to speak, her voice reassuring.

"No darlin', that's the way it's supposed to be when you start out. Just go ahead and brown it in some oil, but it's gonna spark and spit at you a little. Have your slow cooker heated up and when you've done your browning just put it right into the pot. Add your beef broth to it, the potatoes and carrots and onions... just put all of that right into the pot. When that roast is done it will cut like butter, I promise."

Michelle's description made Valentina's stomach growl. This was a different way of cooking for her, but she never doubted her friend's abilities in the kitchen. She let out a relieved sigh. "Oh, that sounds wonderful. Thank you, Michelle. I think I had better get to work on it. I'll see you later, *ciao*."

With that handled, Valentina set about getting the roast prepared and into the slow cooker. She cut up her vegetables and added them as well, then covered all of it with beef broth. Later, she would add a bit of Merlot, the same one she would serve with the meal. Her butternut squash

soup could be made later, as could the bread. She just needed to get home by two o'clock to finish up those items. In the meantime, she intended to find out about funeral arrangements for Doris. Valentina thought again about the woman's husband and wondered if there were children to help attend to him.

It was nine-thirty by the time Valentina was able to get her kitchen cleaned up and head out to run her errands. She wanted to buy some fresh flowers from the new florist whose shop had opened in the expanded marketplace by the general store in Long Lakes' common area. There were entrepreneurs in Long Lakes whose combined efforts had resulted in a co-op of store fronts. The woman who owned the florist shop, Kathy Evans, grew most of the flowers on her property. Valentina intended to choose the flowers for an arrangement that Kathy would make for her to pick up later in the day.

One of the other new shops was a small bakery. It was fast becoming a very popular spot for the locals, and on this day there were tables out on the front porch that ran the length of the building. Every business had a spot for customers to sit outside and enjoy being a part of the community.

The aroma of something wonderful met Valentina as she stepped into the Bakers and Friends shop. She stepped up to the counter and was greeted by the owner, Lizbeth Owens. Her daughter Stephanie was busy refilling the case with the second batch of goodies this morning.

"Hello, Valentina, how nice to see you this morning." Lizbeth's smile was infectious, and Valentina replied with a smile to match it.

"Good morning, what an amazing aroma in here. What is it?"

In reply, Stephanie handed a sample to her. Over the past months, they had become friendly, because they would always arrive at the stables at the same time. They often rode together, now. Valentina couldn't resist making friends with another horse lover.

"Mmmm... this is so good! The frosting is... caramel?"

Lizbeth and Stephanie smiled and nodded.

"Yes, it's called penuche, a brown sugar frosting that is a sort of caramel. The cake is a Kentucky Jam Cake. Do you like it?" Lizbeth said with pride.

Valentina savored every bite and knew Jack's sweet tooth would simply adore it. She decided it would be a perfect way to top off the night's meal.

"Yes, and I would like to buy some for a special dinner I am preparing tonight. How many pieces should I have?"

Lizbeth said,

"What about one slice for each person, plus one extra. It's a rich cake, but..." "One extra piece for seconds. Yes, that sounds perfect. I'll have three slices, please." With two errands completed and one to go, Valentina decided to stop in at the little

restaurant inside the general store. She did like one thing in particular, a Southern delicacy that she had grown to enjoy, but not too often.

Entering the store, Valentina noticed some new items, a nod to the gourmands who were beginning to move into the Long Lakes community. Word had gotten around that this was a very nice place to live, and it was attracting retirees with a measure of wealth as well as younger people who were already tired of city living. Working remotely was now commonplace, so living in a semi-rural setting was a plausible choice for many.

Ellie, the first person to greet everyone, called out to Valentina as soon as she walked through the door. When Jack had arrived in Long Lakes, it had been Ellie who had first welcomed him— almost too much. Ellie had no doubt been disappointed, but not surprised, when it became apparent that he was destined for someone else.

"Hi, Valentina. What brings you in today?" Ellie was a very curious girl, always ready to hear the latest gossip, or share some. Likely, she wanted to hear Valentina's version of what had happened the night before.

Valentina knew she was in for an interrogation regarding Doris. Surely, gossip-hound Lola had alerted most people to the tragic news? Still, while there were several favorite activities in Long Lakes, gossip was at the top of the list.

"Ellie, how are you today? I'm sure you heard about Doris. I am wondering when the funeral will be. Do you know?"

That deflated the woman somewhat, who probably was counting on hearing details, not giving them out.

"Oh, poor Doris. I don't know any details, but I imagine there will be news about all of it. Such a shame..." Ellie let that hang in the air, as if she was waiting for Valentina to give her own details. When Valentina didn't add anything, she carried on.

"So, what can I do for you?"

"I am famished, and I think one of your pimiento cheese sandwiches, grilled, will make me feel very happy." Valentina winked. One thing she had learned about Ellie, a compliment went a long way.

"Ooohh... that does sound good. I'll fix one for you and another one for me!" She burst out laughing.

Valentina found an empty table and sat down, checking her watch to make certain she was on schedule. After she'd eaten, the flowers would be ready, and she could go back to the bakery and pick up her order of Kentucky Jam Cake. What a fun name, something new for her journey of discovery here in America.

Ellie delivered lunch to Valentina, the grilled pimiento cheese sandwich and some potato chips. It had seemed appropriate to drink some Southern sweet tea along with such a classic dish, so she raised her glass to no one in particular.

"*Buon appetito!*" Valentina smiled at Ellie, who practically skipped back to her counter in appreciation for having been included in such a special moment.

Before she finished her lunch, Valentina's cell phone rang. It was on the table already, a habit she'd gotten into after missing too many calls while rummaging through her oversized bag in search of it. To her delight, she saw Jack's name.

"*Ciao, amore!*" Her heart was suddenly beating so fast she was almost breathless. "Hello, my sweet. Look, I'm just now landing in Nashville. By the time I get through picking up my luggage and my car, it's going to be at least two-thirty. I need to stop in at my place and then I'll head for Long Lakes. I should be there around five o'clock. Will that be alright?" Valentina's heart beat a little faster as she heard him say, "Have I told you that I missed you?" "Oh, I missed you too. Five o'clock is fine, we can relax a little before dinner. I can't wait to see you." Valentina felt like a silly schoolgirl, but she didn't care. Just a few more hours until Jack's arms wrapped around her.

"Okay then, see you in a few. Love you."

"Love you. *Ciao.*"

Valentina sighed for the fourth or fifth time that day. That's what love did. The next few hours went by quickly for Valentina. She finished her errands at the marketplace before heading home, carefully placing the flower arrangement she had ordered and the cake box in a larger container made for carrying groceries or packages in the trunk or back seat of a vehicle. It would keep everything safe for the trip home.

Valentina had been keeping to her schedule all day, and when she opened her front door, she could hear her phone alarm dinging that it was two o'clock. She shushed her barking dogs, promising to reward them with a treat. Understanding what the word *treat* meant, they both settled down obediently to wait for it.

Her arms were full, but the kitchen counter accepted everything; the flowers and the bakery box were placed on the counter. She dropped her purse onto a chair placed by the door just for that purpose. With that accomplished, Valentina launched into the final preparations for dinner.

She decided to skip the soup, since the aroma of the roast and vegetables in the slow cooker were too inviting to not make it the star of the evening. Now it was just a matter of mixing the ingredients for her cheese bread and setting it aside to rise. Since Jack would be there at around five o'clock, Valentina would wait to put it in the oven when he arrived. She wanted the luscious bread to be hot when she served it, slathered in butter and completely irresistible.

At three-thirty, she had just enough time to get showered and changed before she set the table and opened two bottles of wine. The Merlot was going to be perfect with this meal, and for sitting by the fire as the evening wore on.

Valentina thought back to life here in Long Lakes, to the time before she met Jack. Life was better now, and with the prospect of their reunion she felt as though tonight could the beginning of another, even better chapter in their lives.

CHAPTER 4

While Valentina got busy on her day's errands, Jack was having thoughts of a different nature. He had been concerned for some time about the dangerous incidents he and Valentina had encountered. Perhaps it was somehow the result of his professional life that she had been at risk on more than one occasion since the two of them met. His life in the FBI was not normally one that included violence, and yet it had come at the two of them head on. He worried that it was his fault somehow. Jack knew that he could not allow his job to be a danger to Valentina. He cared so deeply for her that he would rather quit his job than endanger her again.

The case Jack had been investigating in Dallas was now closed, and his flight back to Tennessee would land in Nashville at around two o'clock in the afternoon. It would give him just enough time to repack his bag before heading to Long Lakes.

To Valentina.

He checked his information once again before leaving his hotel room at nine-thirty, gulping down the last of his morning coffee. Jack would need to return his rental car, a simple drop-off that included a ride to the terminal. Because of his FBI status, Jack was carrying his weapon and able to pass through a security checkpoint especially for Air Marshalls and other legally armed federal employees.

Jack took a seat in what served as business section on the dual class Embraer 170. It was a comfortable plane, well suited for the short flights between major business centers like the one he was making from Dallas to Nashville. The time would be spent considering whether to speak to Valentina about the concerns he had for her safety. Jack couldn't ignore his feelings for her, but he was not going to put her in the line of fire either. He didn't see any answers for this situation that wouldn't cause a disruption of their romance.

But it was more than a romance. Now, it was a relation-ship. It was the only one he'd had since his divorce. Just the thought of his family, of his children, made him worry. Jack loved being an FBI agent, although he would never admit the Fraud Division was not his ultimate career goal.

He'd ventured into the unknown just a little when he considered the possibility of transferring to

a different division, perhaps one that would let him track down criminals like those he had when exposing the drug ring with Valentina.

And then he was back where he started, wondering if his job had put the woman he loved in danger. The rest of the flight back to Nashville was filled with scenarios in which he discussed all of this with Valentina. None of them turned out well.

The perfect autumn day greeted Jack as he made his way out of the Nashville International Airport and headed towards home. The temperatures were already cooling, carrying the crispness that always seemed to accompany the change of seasons this time of year. As his car sailed along the highway, Jack continued the internal discussion that was plaguing him. He visualized Valentina now as his thoughts about her began to battle in earnest.

In the middle of these troubling thoughts, his phone rang. He pushed the answer button on his dashboard and heard his son's voice in response to his own hello.

"Daddy, I made the team! I'm gonna play soccer." Brayden's voice held all the excitement of a young boy advancing to yet another stage of his life.

"Brayden, that's awesome news, son. When is your first game?"

A pang of guilt hit Jack as he thought once more of how much he was missing his children. Lily was growing up into a lovely young girl, and he wondered if he would be there for her to meet a boyfriend or take pictures for her first dance.

Before Brayden could answer Jack's question, the sound of Yvonne wrestling the phone from her son's hand caused another sort of pang. A sort of dread came over him at the sound of her voice.

"Jack, you're going to need to be with the kids this week-end. I have plans and you... well, you need to do your part."

Just like that, the exuberance of talking to Brayden was quelled by the harsh tone of Yvonne's demands. "Yvonne, how nice to hear from you." He unconsciously grimaced at his sarcasm. "I'd love to take the kids, I always love to be with them. What's your big event?"

She let out a long exhale. Jack knew that on the other end of this call, his ex was finding it difficult to not blow up, just because she could. "Marc and I are taking a break, going to the Smokies for a few days to unwind and just be together... alone. I would prefer that you come and stay with the kids here. Brayden's first game is on Saturday and Lily has a sleepover that night. You just need to be here."

He and Valentina would have planned on something this weekend, but he couldn't turn down the opportunity to spend it with his kids. He'd already missed too much over the past few years, and he loved the prospect of being with his son as he embarked on this new activity. "I'll be there. When do you guys leave?"

Jack could practically hear Yvonne's smile. She saw it as some sort of victory, but for Jack it was a godsend. Perhaps he needed to start pulling away from Valentina, and there was no better reason than spending time with the two people to whom he had pledged his heart from the moment they were born.

"Well, we're hoping to get away Friday afternoon. Can you be here by three o'clock? I'll place an order for some pizza to be delivered around five."

"Not a problem. Tell the kids I love them and will see them on Friday. Please. And Yvonne, I really do hope that you and Marc have a good time."

That seemed to cause a slight pause in her reply. They rarely had pleasant conversations anymore, so he might have shocked her. Her response was softer, more like the woman Jack had married.

"I will, Jack, and... I know we've had our issues, but I'm glad you'll have some time here to make memories with our children." Jack heard the change in her voice. "Thanks, I'll see you on Friday. Bye."

Jack muttered his own goodbye as he pressed 'Hang Up' on the dash.

The rest of the drive to his Nashville apartment was spent alternately thinking of Valentina and his children. He loved all of them, but being a father trumped everything. There was a delay on the interstate, and even though he lived close to the busy airport, the constant never-ending roadwork always made the trip longer. Jack was relieved when his exit finally appeared. He swung onto the ramp and eased into the street traffic that would take him home.

As he pulled into his parking space, his thoughts went once more to Valentina. He couldn't wait to see her, to put his arms around her slim body he had grown to know intimately. He knew

the kiss would be ardent, his desire for her not dimmed by his recent worries about her safety. To the contrary, the more he worried, the more deeply he felt his love for her. As soon as he went inside his place, Jack's attention turned to preparing for his trip to Long Lakes. He needed clothes for two days so he chose a pair of jeans and two long-sleeved T-shirts. On the off-chance that he and Valentina would go out one evening, he packed a pale blue button down polo shirt. His leather jacket would work everywhere. While in Dallas, Jack had bought a small gift for Valentina that he put in his duffle bag. It was a small blown-glass figurine of a horse; he was confident she would like it, given her love of horses.

After a shower and change of clothes, Jack was on his way out when his cell began to buzz. It was Yvonne again.

"Hey, what's up?" Had she changed her mind about him coming to stay with the kids? "Dad? It's me, Lily."

Her voice brought a big smile to Jack's face. This girl was his heart. "Hi, sweetie. What can I do for you?"

Once again, Jack pictured his daughter growing up and experiencing each new event in her life. It was a sobering image for a father.

"I just wanted to tell you that I'm so glad you're going to come and stay the weekend. Even if I'm going to a sleep-over, I'll come home early on Sunday. I love you, Daddy." Jack's heart could have burst with love and happiness hearing those words. "I love you too, Lily. We'll have a special breakfast on Sunday, and I can't wait to see you and Brayden. We're going to have a good time, I promise."

Lily blew kisses and said her goodbye. Jack looked at his phone as Yvonne's picture faded from the phone's screen. He needed to make some hard decisions.

The drive included more of the notorious Nashville traffic until he got out of the city and was heading east through open countryside. It was a good time to think, although Jack remained conflicted about being a catalyst for danger to Valentina and possibly his family. After thirty minutes, he decided music was the antidote to too much thinking. Setting his iTunes on shuffle, Jack sang and tapped out rhythms to the music until finally he found himself knocking on the door to Valentina's log house. It was a perfect structure for the surroundings, and like so many

of the other homes in this community it reflected the environment without detracting from it. He really did like it here in Long Lakes. He probably liked it a bit more because of the woman who answered the door.

"Jack! *Finalmente!*" Valentina stepped forward and threw her arms around him, delivering the kiss he had imagined. Jack picked her up and carried her back inside, kicking the door closed as he deepened the kiss with equal portions of love and lust. Everything about Valentina made him want to leave the world behind; it was like a temporary madness that he endured every time they were together.

When their lips finally parted, Jack set her back on her feet. Her hands were around his waist now, holding on as he searched her eyes and kissed her again. This woman... "*Amore mio,* I thought you would never arrive here. I have thought of nothing else all day." Valentina caressed Jack's face with one hand while she rested the other on his chest. "Your heart, it is beating so fast."

Her smile was intoxicating, and Jack felt like a man who'd been in the desert for days. All his intentions to draw away from her were gone in a moment. How could he not be with Valentina? "I'm just so glad to be here." His smile made her own heart skip a beat. "Wow, it smells wonderful in here. What's for dinner?"

That brought another smile to Valentina's face, since he knew she adored cooking for the people she loved. She had opened the wine already, and with another quick kiss, she turned to gather the bottle and two wine glasses. "Tonight you will eat like a king! But first, let's have some wine and you tell me what happened in Dallas."

The evening was chilly enough to light the fireplace, and after their meal and some earnest catching up, the two sat down with their dessert and a cup of coffee to enjoy the warmth. As they did, Jack shared the plans he had made for the weekend.

"I'm really looking forward to being with the kids, it doesn't happen often enough." Jack's tone was almost wistful; his obvious pleasure at the prospect of being with the children was a clear indication of his desire for it to be permanent. Jack was a good father, and he obviously felt the lack of family as things were now.

"I'm so glad for you, I know you miss them. Would you ever be able to get custody again, or partial custody? That would be it, yes?"

Jack nodded, then shook his head. "I don't think I can, at least not if I'm not living closer to them. Plus my job, it's part of the reason we ended up like this."

Valentina put her hand over his, prompting Jack to pull it onto his chest. "Do you think you could ever... I mean... Never mind. I will miss you this weekend, it would have been nice to spend more time together. Perhaps one of these days you will introduce me to Lily and Brayden."

Her smile wasn't met with one from Jack. It disturbed Jack to think he might not want her to meet his children.

Jack needed to let this rest for a bit. It seemed silly to announce that Valentina was in danger from his work on fraud cases. But pulling away, having weekends with his children, that was enough for now. At least this weekend he had a reason to be away, and time to think about all of it.

"Wow, I'm bushed. Your excellent cooking skills must include a recipe for relaxation." Jack stood up and stretched. Valentina was seated on a big floor pillow, and when she looked up at him he bent over and kissed her, feeling aroused by how beautiful she looked by the light of the fire. He didn't want to leave her, not tonight, not ever.

"I am feeling just how long this day has been. Do you mind if I go upstairs?"

Valentina smiled, extending her arm so that Jack could help her up. "I think that is a good idea, you look exhausted."

She got up and took their dishes into the kitchen, quickly rinsed them and added to what was already in the dishwasher. She needed to finish cleaning up, and Jack knew her well enough to recognize that she was still thinking about what he had said. He also knew she hated a dirty kitchen first thing in the morning.

"Why don't you go on upstairs while I clean up here? It won't take me long at all, and you look like you're already half asleep."

Jack didn't argue with her, pausing before his trek upstairs to give her another kiss. "Everything was wonderful. You are wonderful." He kissed Valentina again, and this one was

longer, more suggestive. It was an invitation to make love, and he chastised himself for letting his need for her override his duty to protect her.

How was he supposed to let go of the woman he couldn't live without?

CHAPTER 5

John Watson awoke to a soft snoring, coming from Sherlock. The big black Maine Coon was snuggled beneath a throw blanket reserved especially for him. The two of them had been out late the previous night. The delightful evening spent with Michelle had ended around midnight, and after a nightcap of bourbon (a gift from Michelle), the crisp autumn air had lulled them both into a deep sleep. Waking now to the first rays of sunlight peeking through John's plantation blinds made the sleepy Englishman yearn for a big pot of tea and some friendly room service.

"Nothing to be done about that, my boy, better be up and at it now." At the sound of John's voice, the amiable feline stretched to his full length before crawling out from beneath his blanket. John and Sherlock headed into the kitchen to put on a kettle of water for the morning beverage. Earl Grey would do the trick, and so the morning rituals began.

John decided to have his tea on the screened porch, one of his favorite features of the house. Living in Long Lakes had certainly changed his life, and in all the best ways. He had made friends here, and most importantly he was so very fond of Michelle. She was a woman whose heart was kind and loving, and she filled his own heart completely. Their time together eased the grief of being a widower, filled up the loneliness with what he could only describe as joy. John was content in this house, and he wondered why he had ever sought out love or companionship on a dating website.

The thought of that short episode nearly made John shudder. While participating in activities and building new relationships in the community, John had completely ignored the new remarks and requests that had been coming through in his emails. Only yesterday, another email had arrived, from a place called Happy Matches.

The tea was cold, time for a warmup. The sunlight was that particular shade of gold that only appeared in the early days of autumn. In the South, there were still days of ideal temperatures to accompany the arrival of the season, but the look and feel of fall was present. John walked back into the kitchen and poured some hot water into his mug for a second round of the Earl Grey. Sherlock was still on the porch soaking up the early morning sun as John returned with his laptop in hand.

"Sherlock, my friend, I am going to formally end my adventures with online dating, and it's long overdue."

The look he received from the big cat was one of complete disinterest, bringing a smile to John's face as he considered that Sherlock would never need a matchmaker. He was permanently disengaged from romance.

John opened the notification from Happy Matches to see a long list of messages. He hadn't looked at this for months, not since he first met Michelle. She'd had his heart from the moment he met her. Still, he owed it to himself and the ladies who had sought him out to be courteous enough to decline their interest in him.

John scrolled through, amazed at how many women had been interested in him. Of course, it was normal for people on these sites to respond to multiple profiles, but he could not fathom that so many of them had sought him out. He felt obliged to decline their interest, good manners being of utmost importance to him.

He decided to start from the earliest messages, since they had waited for a response the longest. He went through, giving them all the same short but kind note of rejection. When he reached the third name on the list, though, he paused, and his blood ran cold. It was the very same woman whose dead body he had found two days ago.

"Doris?" Sherlock looked up as he heard her name. John's fingers trembled on the trackpad. It disturbed him to think that he had this in common with her, although he wasn't quite sure why. The inquiry was dated two months earlier, just a few days after he and Michelle had met. "My word..." John thought back to the occasions when he had encountered Doris at Long Lakes. Why had she never mentioned it? Come to think of it, he had seen her once in the company of a man, so perhaps her interest in him was inconsequential. Still, it was eerie to think that if Michelle hadn't come into the picture, they might have dated.

"It's a mystery, Sherlock."

The *mroww* John received in reply to that statement was somehow consoling, as though the cat agreed and would help him deal with it. He continued writing his notes of rejection, and was making good progress until he arrived at one for which he received an immediate reply that the woman was deceased.

"Deceased? Oh, goodness."

It was clearly an automated reply, intended to keep the account from receiving inquiries, but probably a painful reminder to family members that she was now gone.

"Hmmm, Marilyn Durbin. I wonder about the cause of death," he said, reading the name. John tended to talk aloud, a common tendency among those who lived alone. Sherlock was a good sounding board but try as he might the only thing that came out of his mouth was *mroww*. John smiled absentmindedly at his companion's continuing pursuit of the English language.

He clicked on her profile. Marilyn Durbin apparently had family, whereas Doris's profile was still active. He hadn't known much about Doris's life, except that her husband was in a long-term care facility and not expected to ever leave it. Perhaps they never had children, but if he needed more information, it would be easily accessed by a conversation with Lola.

He felt a slight pang of hunger, and realized he could do with another cup of tea. He closed the laptop so Sherlock wouldn't try out his typing skills again. The cat was smart, and he had watched John type enough times to be curious about trying it himself. John was careful now to not give him opportunity, a lesson learned some time ago.

The pantry was full, and at the top of his breakfast list was a gift from Michelle; a luscious loaf of banana bread she had sent home with him last night. John toasted it a bit and then topped it with orange marmalade, his favorite. He put it on a patterned appetizer plate and carried it and a steaming cup of the Earl Grey back to his spot on the porch. Sherlock hadn't moved; he seemed entirely intoxicated by the warmth coming from the rising sun.

John munched on his banana bread, finishing the last bite with a sip of tea. He certainly didn't love Michelle only for her excellent cooking skills, but her talents in the kitchen prompted John to make a mental note of appreciation for this breakfast treat. Setting aside the cup and plate, John opened the laptop again, having decided to try and track down an obituary for Marilyn Durbin. He wasn't sure why, but there was a niggling sensation in the back of his brain that propelled his curiosity. It took a bit of googling, but finally he found a small announcement in *The Knoxville New Sentinel.* It read:

Funeral services for the late Mrs. Marilyn Durbin will be held at Pinehurst Funeral Home in Knoxville on Thursday, November 4 at two o'clock in the afternoon. Mrs. Durbin is the wife of

Steve Durbin, a resident of Silver Springs Residential Care. She is survived by a brother, Steven Murdock, of Chattanooga.

It didn't take long for John to see a similarity with Doris. Both women were childless, and each of their husbands was in a long-term care facility. Was it a coincidence? Sherlock offered a comment by way of a grunt, the sort that cats make in lieu of meowing.

"I think you're right, old man. It is *too much* of a coincidence to be a coincidence." John tapped his chin, intent now on finding out as much as possible concerning the deaths of both Doris and Marilyn. Both women had sought him out at the beginning of his dalliance with online dating. Now, to his dismay, they were both dead. He googled a bit more, searching for a news story about Marilyn Durbin, until he finally landed on an article about her and the business she had begun after her husband's placement in the Silver Springs facility. From the article, he was able to learn her cause of death. An accident. A chill went down his back; yet another disturbing similarity in the stories of the two women.

"Well, dear Sherlock, it appears there might be a problem brewing." Once again, Sherlock chimed in with his opinion, to which John immediately took the advice to heart as he determined to call Michelle.

John got up and took his dishes back into the kitchen. He rinsed them and placed them in the dishwasher, wiped off the counter and tossed the teabag into a container to dry. He would add the contents of it to the rosebush, a trick he had learned from his late wife. The American Beauty in his front yard had been dug up out of her garden and brought here to Long Lakes, burying his grief when he planted the rose bush she had nurtured and loved. The daily ritual of saving his teabag was not out of a desire to live in the past; rather it was an homage to the beautiful life they had lived as husband and wife. It was a good memory, and the roses were a lovely reminder that one's past could be remembered without being consumed by it.

After finishing up in the kitchen, John sat down with his phone in hand and rang Michelle. She answered on the second ring. "Hello, John, and good morning to you." The sweet Southern drawl was like a balm to the British ex-pat.

"Good morning, my dear. Do you have time for me to drop by this morning? I have something I need to share with you, a discovery I have made... Well, I don't want to go into it over the phone.

What do you say, I'm just tidying up a bit here but I can come over whenever it is convenient for you." To be honest, John would have come up with some other reason to see Michelle if he hadn't had a real incentive with what he had discovered about the women.

"Sugar, you are always welcome in my home. Why don't you come over around eleven and I'll fix us some lunch."

John liked the sound of that, and he couldn't help but smile at the affection intoned with the use of *sugar*. It was a charming Southernism to which he was becoming especially attached. "That sounds marvelous, and I shall gladly let you feed me! You know you're spoiling me with such good food, I believe I may have put on a few pounds since eating at your table."

He meant it, but it was worth it to be near this woman. Perhaps he could take up walking in earnest. "I shall be there at eleven. Until then, my sweet." John figured that was the English equivalent of calling someone '*sugar*'. He had a new appreciation for endearments since living in the South.

The call ended and John set about finishing up a few tasks, the last being a shower. Sherlock was waiting outside the bathroom door when he emerged, a behavior typical for him. There was a fresh set of clothes set out that reflected the change in the weather. It wasn't very cold outside, but with a slight drop in temperature, John added a sweater vest.

John had always worn a bow tie; it had been a particularly favorite accessory down through the years. He put one on now, a black one to complement the colors in the plaid shirt he was wearing. Thanks to a shopping trip with Michelle, John was wearing blue jeans for the first time in quite a while. No point in looking doddery, and if Michelle liked them, well he'd wear them, by golly. He stepped into his Doc Martens suede Oxfords (made in England, thank you very much), and then checked out his reflection in the oversized full-length mirror leaning against the wall opposite his bed. He took it all in, complimenting himself on what he saw. He might have been over sixty, but he could still clean up pretty well. Michelle had helped him with this ensemble, and he hoped it would please her to see him in it.

When John emerged from his house, he took in a big breath of the crisp air, grateful that the chill of it was mostly gone as the sun had done its work to warm things up. Sherlock was content to remain inside and finish his napping. A cat who enjoyed a routine was also a creature of whim,

and John recognized that and bade his loyal friend adieu as he closed the door behind him. The walk to Michelle's would take about twenty minutes, and considering his anticipation of a filling meal, he opted to walk rather than drive. The two of them had talked about bicycling around the community, and with each step he resolved to purchase a suitable bicycle for that very activity. When John had arrived in Long Lakes, he was looking a little worse for wear, he reckoned. He was neat and tidy, to be sure, but he made no boast of being stylish, save for the bow tie. Michelle was a tad younger than he, and although she never seemed to want him to change in any way, the suggestion of blue jeans was something he decided to act on. Arriving at her front door, John felt up to the task of dating a slightly younger woman. He also felt the excitement of discussing his discovery concerning the two women who had shown an interest in dating him, and who were now both dead.

There was more to this than anyone suspected. Of that he was certain.

CHAPTER 6

The intoxicating aroma of fresh baked bread and roast chicken filled Michelle's kitchen, melding with the homey interior that spoke a welcome to anyone fortunate enough to walk through her front door. It was a gift, and it partially defined this Southern woman in her relationships, especially the close ones. The one she was sharing with John Watson qualified as close, nearing a state of intimacy that would herald an entirely new level of hospitality for someone who had been single for more than a few years.

"Oh, lord have mercy!" Michelle responded to sound of her doorbell, hoping for the umpteenth time that her hair looked right and her blouse wasn't too tight. In fact, much to her delight, Michelle had lost ten pounds since she had been seeing John. That was always a good sign, being too infatuated with a man to want to eat. It seemed her metabolism always charged up considerably when love wafted by.

There were fresh flowers on the dining table, candles burning on the fireplace mantle and, most importantly, that luscious pan-roasted hen in the oven, saturated in butter and rosemary. Au gratin potatoes and glazed carrots were the side attractions, but first would be her salad of mixed greens (the last of her own summer garden), dotted with berries and walnuts and topped with a beautiful balsamic and honey dressing. If food was the way to a man's heart, Michelle had little doubt that John's would be hers alone.

Michelle opened the front door with a flourish, fully expecting to see John standing there on the porch. Instead, surprising her but not unwelcome, was Valentina.

The unexpected visitor must have seen a fleeting expression of disappointment, because she hurriedly explaining why she was there. "Oh, you are expecting... John? I only need to borrow something, some cornstarch if you have extra."

Michelle smiled and invited Valentina inside. "Let me get that, of course you can always borrow anything you need. And yes, John is coming down for lunch and, well, you know." She winked at her friend, although to this point in her relationship with John there hadn't been any real physical intimacy. They were both cautious, and perhaps a little shy.

Michelle put some of the cornstarch into a baggie and handed it to the curious woman who had become her best friend here in Long Lakes. She would never have dreamt that she could find real friendship here and, possibly even love.

"Here you go. What's this going into?" Both women were excellent home cooks, and they often exchanged dishes with one another, sharing their recipes and making time for catching up or sharing news. Valentina sighed before answering, which was concerning. Something was on her friend's mind. Michelle made a note to ask more about that later, since John would be there momentarily.

Just as she thought that, the doorbell chimed.

"Oh no, I've stayed too long. That must be John now." Valentina made a beeline for the door with Michelle close behind. When the door opened, it was John, and his surprise at seeing both women caught him slightly off guard.

"John, come on in, sugar." The endearment slipped out of Michelle's mouth before she could think about it.

Valentina slid past the two older people and waved as she trotted down the walkway. John came inside and inhaled deeply the smell wafting from the kitchen. "Ah." As Michelle took his hand, the oven timer rang, announcing that lunch would soon be on the table. She pointed him towards it and urged him to sit down, which he did willingly and with great anticipation.

Michelle was able to get everything on the table without a hitch, and John eagerly filled his plate and then looked at it with a degree of awe. It was beautiful, and the salad bowl glistened with the berries and vinaigrette.

"You are an artist, my dear."

Michelle thought she might be glowing just a little; it was something she just naturally did but it pleased her no end to hear John acknowledge it.

The meal was unhurried, and the conversation went from reviews of their respective days and finally, inevitably, to the scene at Doris's house two nights ago. Each of them had a limited acquaintance with the woman, but her death had affected them as though she were a close friend. But then John began to tell her that Doris had once contacted him through the online

dating agency, Happy Matches. Michelle already knew that John had engaged the service before moving to Long Lakes, so that when he brought it up, there were no surprises. None, that is, until he revealed the news of Doris's inquiry into his account.

"John, do you mean to tell me that you and Doris...?"

"No, no, that did not occur. She only inquired. But, there is more to it."

One of the things that Michelle was not quite used to as yet was John's habit of introducing a topic or point of conversation, and then letting it hang in the air without explanation. As she waited for the follow-up to his intrigue, her expression betrayed what she was thinking.

"Oh dear, I've done it again. No dramatic pauses, I'll get right to it. Another woman made an inquiry on my, umm... profile. That's what they call it. Another woman who has also died." He waited for a response, but Michelle didn't seem particularly alarmed. "Did you hear me? Two women, each of whom contacted me through this dating agency, are now dead. I find that particularly curious."

Michelle was thinking about it, running scenarios through her mind about John and a throng of other women who wanted him. But then his point began to penetrate her thinking and she was struck by the peculiarity of it.

Then again, it was likely John attracted older women. And older women, unfortunately, died. "Who is the other woman? Where did she live?"

"The second woman, well she actually passed before Doris... her name is Marilyn Durbin, of Knoxville. There was no cause of death listed in the obituary. But she too was the wife of a man in a convalescent facility and had no children."

"You don't know how she died?"

"From the obituary, it appeared to be sudden. An accident, possibly."

Now the picture was beginning to sharpen as Michelle considered the probability of two such similar circumstances. Was John the key to this, somehow? If John wasn't the connection, then someone or something else had to be.

"Do you think, I mean is it possible that this dating website is somehow involved? This is a real mystery, and somehow you're in the middle of it."

"It certainly seems that way."

Michelle had a sudden pang of concern for John. Was he in danger? "Should we go to the police with this? Darlin', what if you are a target of something dangerous?" The two of them shared a slight shiver down their spines, a dawning of realization that perhaps these two women had been murdered. Michelle and John continued to talk about the mystery of the two deaths and how they were connected to him. As they finished their meal, the scene shifted to the living room and a cup of tea to go with shortbread cookies. Michelle had an idea brewing alongside the kettle, enough so that when she brought in a tray with the tea and cookies they were accompanied by a scheme to try and catch a killer.

"John, what if I were to join this dating site and…" She saw the look on John's face and realized he was already thinking the same thing.

The difference was, Michelle saw disapproval.

"Wait a minute, let me just say it out loud. What if we look at what those two women said about themselves, and then I join and put down the same sort of things. Whatever it is they had in common, which seems to be their invalid husbands, then I'll just do the same. I can use an alias, that way they can't find me or look me up."

The conversation about creating a plan to investigate went on for several hours, so that when four o'clock rolled around, Michelle switched her plotting to figuring out an evening meal. As she and John offered ideas and scenarios Michelle put together a chicken salad, piling it onto crusty ciabatta bread and topping it with smoked Gouda cheese. It was an open-faced sandwich that she put under the broiler until it was bubbly and golden brown.

By the time John gave Michelle an affectionate kiss goodnight, she was already wondering if they should consult someone else about their plan. And it was a plan. All that it lacked was the execution and some sort of way to deal with what might come of it. Naturally, the person that came to mind was Valentina. Michelle didn't know anyone else she would trust to hold that sort of information. She also knew that there would be objections to going undercover, so to speak. It was too late to call her now, but in the morning, Michelle would have a talk with her friend. For now, bed was calling her, and she intended to answer. By morning, she would have a better picture of her plan.

After she fell asleep, a crashing sound outside on her back porch made Michelle jump. She took a quick look at the clock. It was five-thirty in the too-early morning. What on earth had made that racket? She threw on an oversized sweater that served as a robe, and moved as swiftly as she could considering she was not quite awake. After the conversation last night, the idea of someone coming to stop her from investigating Doris's death seemed all too likely.

From the glass sliding door, Michelle saw the galvanized buckets she had left on the back porch. They were turned over and scuttling around them in what looked to be a scavenger hunt for something to eat, were two pudgy little critters she recognized as hedgehogs. The two were obviously hungry, but what were they doing here? Michelle slid back the sliding door as quietly as possible, not wanting to alarm the two spiny little animals. Hedgehogs were not native to this area, not indeed anywhere in North America. Michelle knew people would buy animals and then abandon them, which may have been the story here. She decided to grab a handful of the blueberries she had left over from her salad the day before, and then slide them as carefully as she could through the narrow opening and out onto the porch. The hedgehogs stood perfectly still, as though that would make them invisible. Michelle put the berries down on the porch and backed up until she was at the door.

The hedgehogs hadn't moved, but now they edged in a little closer to the berries and in one movement, each of them gobbled up roughly a handful of blueberries.

Michelle breathed a sigh of relief, although the last thing she needed was a pair of hedgehogs for pets. Her cat had watched all of this from safe inside the house, sitting in the window to observe the creatures who were stealing attention that rightly belonged to her.

Michelle had to laugh at her visitors. What a strange encounter, but these days she had become used to surprises.

Having successfully gained something akin to trust from the two little chubs, Michelle went back inside to put on some coffee. It was too early to call Valentina, so she set about clearing away the dishes that hadn't been rinsed and put in the dishwasher last night. She had been too weary to wash the roasting pan and so she started on it now while her coffee brewed. She thought about John, and the sweet kiss he had planted on her mouth. She wouldn't have minded

something a little more ardent, a little more of an invitation. But, like herself, he had lost a spouse, and embarking on a love connection was daunting.

She popped the big pan into the dishwasher just as her coffeemaker chimed that it was finished. Michelle took her favorite mug and poured in some half-and-half before filling it with the fresh brew. What a great thing to take that first sip, it was like a big hug.

When the clock struck eight, Michelle decided it was okay to call Valentina. She was excited to talk to her about all that she and John had discussed the night before. Thinking about it again, it was a bit of a rush to consider that they might expose a killer. It was also a little bit scary.

Michelle told Siri to call Valentina, and immediately changed her mind about telling her friend the fantastic tale she and John were considering. *'Settle down girl, there's a right time for everything and now might not be that time.'*

"Michelle? What's up so early?"

"I'm so sorry, did I wake you up? I can call back later."

"No, no it's fine. Jack just left for Nashville. His office called him to help close a case, and I'm having my coffee now, so let's talk."

And with that invitation, Michelle told her friend about the wonderful evening she had spent with her Englishman. Some things would have to wait.

CHAPTER 7

Victory played within the mind of Doris's killer. The simplicity of the execution, the whimper of realization that death and darkness were total and unavoidable.

Sitting in the sunny room above a revitalized area on Gay Street in Knoxville's historic district, the memories of this event joined other similar victories in the pursuit of happiness. It was a pursuit that had proved futile for Doris, whose indiscretions and selfish motives had ultimately betrayed her.

A jangling noise from outside disturbed his reverie. These were altruistic deeds, pure and simple. Vows of love and devotion seemed a thing of the past, and a cavalier disregard for those vows could lead others like Doris to the same sort of sin, and the same sort of death.

The mission was to save them before they committed the ultimate act of unfaithfulness. It was better to die without the stain of sin than enter an unholy alliance. Thoughts of Henry VIII and Anne Boleyn often came to mind; the queen whose guilt was presumed but whose death deterred her from the certainty of it. Yes, there was wisdom in execution.

How often were good deeds misconceived as evil? An ounce of prevention, wasn't that the term? Surely a great service was being performed, although admitting to it would prove disastrous. There would be no way to continue this crusade if others knew of it. Sometimes justice required extraordinary measures, and this justice was more than an act of vengeance. Justice could pre-empt a greater offense, intervening before the sin of it completely overwhelmed a person. Saving the offender from committing a greater offense, changing the measure of damage, and leaving only the remembrance of loyalty and love for those who remained.

So far, thankfully, this operation was unrecognized for what it was. Accidents were amazingly easy to create, circumstances easily controlled. Doris had been so distracted by her game that she'd lost all contact with reality, the virtual reality literally changing hers. And there it was, the infatuation with what was not real taking precedence over her reality. Doris was a married woman, with a husband languishing in a never-ending world of disembodiment. The man suffered the loss of his world while Doris pursued respite from her perception of loss. Where was

the love, or the long-suffering mate who had vowed to remain faithful no matter what they encountered? Doris had failed, and although she hadn't gone through with the final act of betrayal, she *would* have. But now, safe in the arms of eternity, she could live on in memory as a loyal and precious wife.

This job was similar to the crusades of superheroes. Shielded by anonymity and stealth, justice could be meted out to those in the wrong. Eventually, the truth might emerge, but by then the message would be a clarion call to the like-minded. *Cheating is bad, and cheaters must be saved from themselves when possible.*

This wasn't a hate crime. Sin was being supplanted with sacrifice.

The phone rang, jolting him from his thoughts. Ignoring the phone, he let himself go back to something more concrete, more real.

Two years ago he had been the victim of deceit and betrayal. His wife had abandoned him to a fate that was unmerited and seemingly irreversible. He had lain comatose for two months, the victim of a mild stroke and, more devastating, his wife's machinations to claim his fortune while her lover oversaw his care. They carried on an affair and he was supposed to wither away and die.

What the lovers hadn't counted on was that he would recover.

That kind of assumption could be fatal. It was a lesson usually learned too late.

CHAPTER 8

J ack waved again to his family as he backed out of
Yvonne's driveway.

His family.

They *were* his family, all of them. Even with a divorce
between him and Yvonne, the bond of their children kept
them connected. Although there had been a lot of water
under the proverbial bridge, her attitude towards him this
weekend had softened, her demeanor welcoming despite
past disputes.

Brayden and Lily waved back and blew kisses as he drove
away, and when he looked in his rear-view mirror, it was
Yvonne who seemed the most affected by the scene.
Perhaps the way her own weekend had gone was the
reason for all of it. She was a woman whose heart could

shift from cold dismissal to warm embraces over a silly argument. The reverse was also true, something that Marc was undoubtedly learning at this very moment.

Jack reviewed the events of the past few days: Brayden's first soccer game and Lily's excitement over a sleepover with her friends. On Sunday morning, Jack had prepared a breakfast that made his kids happy, and it didn't get any better than that for a dad. He needed his children to be happy.

As the memories of the weekend came flooding back to him, Jack wondered if he could accomplish that task of creating a happy life for his children if circumstances were to change. He loved Valentina, but where was the relationship going? She was content in Long Lakes, running her business and being an independent woman. They had never discussed marriage, nor had she made any demands of him regarding that sort of permanence.

Yvonne was a woman who needed marriage, and he had a suspicion about her relationship with Marc that made him think the two of them were hitting a wall. Obviously, the trip to the Smokies had not gone as planned, and Marc's absence when Yvonne returned home seemed to indicate trouble between them. Was it possible that there was a way to gain his family back?

As soon as he thought it, the image of Valentina overtook him; he loved her and in no world of his own choosing would he go back to Yvonne. No, the past was indelibly printed into the

account of his life, and so he must figure out another way to spend more time with his children that didn't involve needing to spend that same time with his ex-wife.

Jack was reasonably content with this resolution until he landed once more on the events in which Valentina's life had been endangered by his involvement in the cases that led to murder. He knew that it wasn't his job that caused those situations, and yet as things had progressed it was his job that intensified the danger. Valentina would always be in the path of harm if he were in the picture. She would be a target for anyone who was Jack's enemy, of that he was certain.

I deal with fraud, it shouldn't even be dangerous.

That thought didn't keep Jack from feeling apprehensive about the danger that was possible. While Valentina was involved with him there was the possibility of her being hurt, and he couldn't bear to be responsible for that happening.

Jack's apartment was only thirty minutes from Yvonne's house. It used to be his house too, and the memories within those walls turned to the awful arguments between them, the attempts to not let the kids know how miserable they each were. He could never go back to that; the seeming truce between them this morning was merely

Yvonne needing someone to reassure her that she wouldn't be alone. The truth of the matter seemed to always go back to the fact that Yvonne created drama, just as she had when she began an affair while they were married. Jack had made mistakes, but before her infidelity sealed their fate, he was willing to try and work things out, to make changes.

How could loving someone as much as he loved Valentina put him on a path to this sort of internal conflict? He was more confused now than when he left his kids in the rearview mirror. The need for something comfortable and filling persuaded him to stop at a local drive-thru to pick up something for dinner. This family-owned restaurant served the best catfish and hushpuppies in the city, at least by Jack's estimation. He placed his order, anticipating that first bite of the cornmeal battered fish. After paying for and picking up his order, the temptation to dig into it was almost too tantalizing to resist. He decided to wait; the idea of being in his own space was beginning to seem a more realistic goal than whatever he had conjured up in the past twenty minutes.

Jack turned into the parking lot of his apartment complex and pulled into his space. He only had an overnight bag to take up, along with his box of catfish. He reached behind his seat to pull the bag from the back seat and headed upstairs. He had never felt like this place was his home, merely a stopping-off place. Valentina's house felt like home to him. The aroma of her cooking and the thoughtfulness of everything she did to make her home a welcoming place gave him a feeling of being valued.

When Jack stepped up to his door, keys in hand, it was obvious that the door was ajar. He dropped his bag, carefully placing his dinner on top of it, and pushed the door all the way open.

"Surprise, baby!"

It was Yvonne, apparently stark naked except for a sheet she had wrapped herself in. Her smile seemed to indicate that she was expecting Jack to like her surprise. "What? How did you get here so fast?" Jack was dumbfounded and slightly scared. He certainly hadn't expected this, but here she was, and with obvious expectations. "Jack, darling, I know we had a spark between us and I want to explore that. We have a family, and we should be together. Don't you agree?"

Jack was speechless. Yvonne could pull off some crazy stunts, but this one would go down as the worst.

"Yvonne, please put your clothes back on. I'm sorry if you got the impression that I wanted this, but... no, I don't think we should be together. And how did you get here so fast?" Jack averted his eyes, as another question came to mind. "Yvonne, where are the children?"

She laughed at the look on Jack's face, "They're at Maddie's, next door. The kids are fine, Jack. You know I wouldn't do anything to hurt them."

When he didn't rush forward to take her, the look on the Yvonne's face changed into a combination of indignation and anger. Jack's own senses went on high-alert; Yvonne's moods were so changeable that she just might do him in for the crime of not wanting her. He added that to the list of things that might endanger Valentina.

Yvonne sat down on the sofa and began to weep uncontrollably, prompting Jack to sit down next to her and put his arm around her bare shoulders. This was a woman whose heart was being

broken, and in an act of desperation she had tried to rekindle a lost part of her life. Between sobs, Yvonne tried to explain herself, but she was too overcome. Jack did his best to console her, but it wouldn't be in the way she had hoped.

"Marc is going to leave me. He's in love with someone else. Oh, Jack, he's doing to me what I did to you. I'm so sorry. I made such a big mistake."

More sobbing and a box of tissues did little to assuage her misery, but Jack sat with her until it finally subsided. "Yvonne, you broke every speed law in Nashville to beat me home. What were you thinking?" He said it with a wink, and finally Yvonne gave him a small smile.

"I was just so upset, and when we seemed to get along so well I just... well, you know. I'm sorry, it isn't fair to you. I think I'm in for a very difficult lesson."

It was at that moment that Jack's phone rang. It was Valentina. He debated about not answering but he really did want to hear her voice.

"Hello," Jack would've called her beautiful, but didn't want to wound Yvonne any deeper; he hoped Valentina could hear the smile on his face.

"Is that the kids?" Yvonne's question must have reached Valentina's ears, because there was a sudden chill of silence on the other end of their call.

"Oh, that is Yvonne. She stopped in to give me something from the kids." One fast lie was better than explaining what was really going on.

What Jack heard from Valentina was a swift goodbye, they would talk later. It grieved him to think that a misunderstanding might come out of this, but perhaps it was a way to slow down their romance. Jack still had concerns about how his job might affect Valentina's safety. Was he being too protective? Maybe there was nothing to it, and he should stop worrying about it. Better to start worrying about her response to Yvonne being in his apartment.

Jack went into his bedroom and found the clothes Yvonne had shed in order to make her dramatic scene come to life.

His bed was now stripped, so he'd have to add that to his list of things to accomplish tonight. And his supper...

"Yvonne, have you eaten anything today? I have some of Roxy's catfish; you're welcome to share." The offer was sincere, but not completely void of concern about what Yvonne might still

be thinking. Jack knew the woman, knew her tactics of manipulation. She was a woman who went after what she wanted, sometimes to her own harm.

"That sounds really good, thank you. I, umm... well, I guess I should get dressed first. Give me a minute."

She turned towards the bedroom and Jack retrieved his bag and the box of fish from his little porch. This was not what he had in mind when he stopped for a bit of comfort food. Over their shared meal, Jack and Yvonne chatted about their children, about how fast they were growing up. Yvonne was a good mother, and Jack appreciated that about her. In truth, he didn't blame her for the breakup of their marriage. He had been consumed with his work and neglectful towards his wife. They created a circumstance that led to hurt and... water under the bridge. Once more, Jack reminded himself of the need not only to be forgiven, but to forgive. "Do you have any plans, any ideas about going back to work?" Jack had always hoped that Yvonne would go back to her career, the one she had left in order to raise their children. "I can't go back to the corporate world. What I've been thinking about is, well… it may sound silly but I'd like to open a little store."

Jack was not entirely surprised; Yvonne was good with merchandising and people, a perfect combination for retail. "What sort of store? It's a pretty competitive market for small retailers." He spoke off the top of his head, since he knew virtually nothing about retail.

Yvonne set down the piece of catfish she was eating and looked into Jack's eyes. "I want to import fine stationery goods from around the world, capitalize on the popularity of paper and personal correspondence that is trending. People are tired of emails and impersonal communication; it's a good time to sell the idea of the romance of writing a letter or posting a personal note in a card. I have made some contacts and looked into a couple of locations."

"Really? Sounds fabulous." She was clearly invested, passionate, and had done her homework.

She looked at Jack more intensely now, imploring him to pay attention. "Would you consider coming to look at the two spaces? I just need another opinion, that's all. If this takes off it is another source of income to help support our children, maybe for the long term."

Jack was interested in the idea. Yvonne had a good head on her shoulders, despite a few tantrums that exposed her less than logical way of looking at some things. This idea seemed like a good one, and the least that he could do would be to help her get started with the right location.

"Of course, I think your idea sounds exciting and potentially something that could be around for years. People will always need to reach each other, and then you have invitations and announcements."

"Oh, Jack, thank you! I was so hopeful that you would approve," she gushed, but then seemed embarrassed at her response. "Oh, you know what I mean. This is not just for me, it's for our children, for their future. If I do this, I mean for it be around for a very long time. Failure is not an option, right?"

Jack smiled at that; he had often used that phrase to encourage her and the kids in things they found difficult. "Yes, you're right. It will be a great success, I have no doubt." The two raised their water bottles in a sign of agreement.

CHAPTER 9

Valentina hung up on Jack with a barely audible 'see you later,' her mind swirling with concerns at the sound of Yvonne's voice in the background. What was she really doing at Jack's apartment? His weak excuse rankled, causing Valentina to doubt the sense of honor and trust in a man she believed loved her. Or was it just hope on her part?

As she continued to ask questions of no one in particular, Valentina heard the chime of her doorbell. She wished in vain that it could be Jack, but apparently he was in Nashville... with Yvonne. No, it was just a delivery for her business.

The rest of the day was filled with updating some account information for one of her stores in Nashville. The wine import business had developed in the process required to immigrate to the United States. It was a moderate success at this point, and its growth was on track for it to be a viable and permanent income for Valentina. This was her way of bringing a little of her homeland to the new home she was adopting.

By four o'clock she was finished with her workday, and as if on a timer, the doorbell chimed. She had just completed the last call of the day, so she put the phone down and went to answer her door, curious now as to who it might be. Valentina looked out onto the porch through her farmhouse door, complete with a paned window in the top portion. She loved this vintage door; it had been one of her prized finds at a restoration warehouse outside of Knoxville. She opened it to Michelle and her gentleman friend, John Watson.

"Hello, you two, what are you up to now?"

She was pleased to see them; it would take her mind off of Jack and Yvonne. Valentina motioned for them to come inside and then led them into her living room. The pair seemed to have something between them, and as soon as they were all seated the story started spilling out. Valentina could barely keep up with their excited explanation.

"Wait a minute, you are telling me that Doris was murdered? How do you know? I think I lost part of your story in all of this excitement. What do you know that the police do not?"

Michelle clutched John's hand and started over. Sometimes she tended to forget that English wasn't her friend's native language, and she did talk fast with a Southern drawl. When she was this excited, Valentina had trouble understanding everything she was saying.

"Valentina, John has discovered a connection between Doris and another woman who was, um... who is dead. They both contacted him for a date." Michelle saw the confusion and explained a bit more. "John was on a dating website before he moved here and, well, before we met. Doris was on the same website, as was another woman who is also dead under similar circumstances. What is her name, dear?"

John cleared his throat and continued the narrative. "Marilyn Durbin also had an account on this website, and like Doris she wasn't exactly single. Both women are survived by husbands who are in assisted living facilities, either in a coma or simply completely incapacitated. Curious, don't you agree?"

Valentina sat back in her chair, having been literally on the edge of her seat as she listened to the accounts about the two deceased women. Yes, very curious.

"So, what is it you propose to do with this knowledge?

Certainly the police will find all of this very interesting, or even discover it themselves, yes?"

John shot Michelle a look that seemed very conspiratorial to Valentina. What were they up to? she wondered, and then it struck her that they were planning their own investigation. "Oh_no, you two must not get involved. If someone has killed these women then you will be putting yourselves at risk," Valentina said, her voice raised in alarm. "Let us call the police and they will sort it out. Haven't we had enough close calls already?" Valentina thought back to the two encounters she had survived with murder and mayhem. Long Lakes was supposed to be her place of peace and serenity, not chasing after criminals and serial killers.

"Oh, John, we've upset her. Valentina dear, please don't worry yourself about this. We're just thinking of placing a phony ad on this dating website. I probably won't even be contacted by anyone."

Michelle might have thought this would make her friend feel better, but instead Valentina shot up out of her chair and pointed a finger at Michelle.

"But it is a dating website. You are going on this website and will do what exactly?" she demanded. First Jack and now this. Everyone was mad, and she felt like it was her job alone to keep a sense of sanity.

John put his arm around Michelle's shoulder and pulled her in close, as if nothing would harm his lady friend. But Valentina knew better.

"You two are crazy if you think you can catch this fellow, if there is a fellow to catch. What makes you think that he would pick you, Michelle? What will you write about yourself to make him take your bait? You are not a fish for him to catch and..." Valentina paused, a bit lost in her attempt to create an analogy. "You simply must not do this. Please."

Michelle got up and hugged Valentina. "Look, Valentina, we won't do anything careless. But if someone does respond then don't you think it's worthwhile to at least investigate it a little bit? John will be with me, and we were hoping you would be as well. I only intend to make a profile using a made-up name and details. I'll say that I'm not looking for anything permanent, just a companion since my poor husband is in a coma or something like that. How many men are looking for someone in that sort of circumstance? We can pass on our suspicions to the police once we have something more concrete."

Valentina could see the logic in this plan. So long as Michelle didn't have to be alone with someone else, perhaps there was something to their madness. "Okay, okay... I will go along with it on one condition. You must never be alone with anyone from this dating service. You must only go to a place where John and I can see you and step in if anything, umm... how do you say it? Hinky, anything hinky happens."

Michelle laughed out loud at the word hinky. "Valentina, where do you find these words? Okay, fine, nothing hinky. You and John are my watchdogs every step of the way." She winked at the Englishman as Valentina relented.

"I still do not like it completely. But if you two are determined then I intend to be with you on it. May I tell Jack about this plan?" Valentina was still upset with Jack having Yvonne in his apartment, but in the long run she would feel better if he were aware of what was going to be transpiring among the three friends. It might not hurt to have the FBI on speed dial in case something happened that needed law enforcement back-up.

She could see that the idea of including Jack was not something that Michelle or John had counted on. They trusted him, but he might not let them proceed with their plan if he were aware of it. Michelle said, "Perhaps we should wait on that, just let me get the profile up and then see if we get any hits. It might all just amount to nothing at all. What do you say?"

Valentina nodded slowly; this might work out and then they could call in the police. Maybe Jack wouldn't be angry with her for doing this behind his back, but she somehow doubted it. Besides, he seemed to be inclined to spend more time with his children. The timing might not be quite right for her to ask him to help with this.

"Sure, I think you are right. This isn't even Jack's line of investigation, so it might be better if we don't interfere with his job."

As much as her heart hurt from it, she wasn't ready to confide in Michelle about her feelings towards Jack and the discovery of Yvonne at his apartment. No, better to set her mind to work on this little dating scheme instead of thinking about how things might be going all wrong with the man she loved.

"So, do we start working on this dating profile? We'll need a picture of you, Michelle, something tempting." Valentina saw John's reaction to that, perhaps a little bit of regret at agreeing to put his new love in the line of another man's affection. There were so many ways that this could go very wrong.

The three conspirators decided to meet again in the morning and do a more thorough plan for this scheme to catch a killer. Valentina was happy enough to let Michelle prepare breakfast for them, and she would bring her laptop and a thumb drive to record everything. They decided they should probably upload everything from a neutral location, but for now, they needed to create a profile that might just entice whoever they were after into pursuing Michelle.

After agreeing to meet at nine o'clock the next morning John took Michelle's hand and led her to the front door. Valentina was so fond of the couple, they were perfect together, a thought that prompted a sigh from her as she walked with them out onto her front porch.

"I had better get home and fix some supper, it's Mahjong night, you know." Michelle put her arm through John's as they walked down to the road and headed back to her home, waving to Valentina.

It was getting dark already, the days were shorter, and the sun had nearly set to its night time resting place. Valentina walked back into the house and through the kitchen. She opened her sliding glass door and let the sounds of the evening serenade her. There were still a few lightning bugs here in the last warm days of autumn. She called in the dogs from their spots on the back porch, preparing a bowl for each of them.

She wasn't very hungry and decided on a nice green salad with olives and mozzarella. She paired that with a light-bodied Pinot Grigio and, remembering there was still a small piece of cake from the night Jack dined with her, Valentina saved the last few sips of wine to go with the Kentucky Jam Cake. Oddly enough, she found the combination pleasing.

She felt restless, and the memory of hearing Yvonne's voice over the phone continued to make her sad, and a little bit angry. Jack had never been unkind about his ex-wife, but Valentina knew she had hurt him by being unfaithful. Jack took responsibility for his part in the failure of the marriage, but the affair had been the last straw. So, what was Yvonne up to, she wondered? A woman's intuition was worth its weight in gold, and right now Valentina was betting on the probability that Yvonne was going to try and win back the man she had driven away. The question was, could she do it?

Valentina decided to go for a walk and try to take her mind off that last brief conversation with Jack. He hadn't even called her back to try and explain. Had Yvonne spent the rest of the day with him? Was that why he hadn't called? She put on her walking shoes and grabbed a light-weight jacket. The air was comfortable, but the temperature would drop a little as the evening wore on. Valentina decided to walk down to the store and see what was going on tonight.

That's when it hit her. It was Monday night. It had been one week exactly since Doris was found. It was Mahjong night, so those ladies, including Michelle, would be there and possibly needing a fourth. Well, it was worth a visit.

The road was good for walking and jogging, and with the temperature just in the mid-sixties, Valentina didn't need the jacket she had tied around her waist. She made the trip in a little less than fifteen minutes, just in time to see the ladies arriving for their Mahjong game. Just as she had figured, there were only the three of them. Either someone had forgotten to ask another to play, or no one was willing to endure an evening with Lola Edwards and her friend Delta Rivers.

Thankfully Michelle was already there, and Valentina wondered briefly that she hadn't asked her to play. Then again, Michelle knew how her friend felt about Lola, so had probably assumed she wouldn't be interested. But tonight, Valentina figured she could endure Lola and Delta if it meant taking her mind off Jack, and maybe doing a little investigating into Doris's life.

Michelle saw Valentina first, and waved at her to come over to their table. She seemed a little surprised, but genuinely glad to see her. "Hello, stranger. What brings you here?" Valentina slid into the only empty chair. "I hope you're not expecting anyone else. I was thinking that perhaps I could join the game. Would that be okay?"

Lola, who was just taking her seat, practically purred her delight at having the Italian woman at the table. "Dear sweet Valentina, you are welcome at our table. You know we're missing our dear Doris, such a pity." She clucked her tongue, emphasizing how sad she was to lose a friend.

Delta Rivers, who was apparently so named because of the place she was born near the Mississippi River, across from

Memphis, was a stranger to Valentina but welcomed her with a smile.

"I have been wantin' to meet you. You run that wine business, don't ya? I just love a good muscadine wine, do you have any of that?"

"I'm afraid not, I only import wines from Italy. I don't think I have ever had muscadine wine." She had a puzzled look on her face, but then there were still so many things in America that were a mystery to her.

"Oh, well then I'll have to find some myself and let you try it. It's sweet and... oh my, it's like the nectar of the gods. That's what my granddaddy used to say, nectar of the gods." She took on a wistful expression as if caught in the memory of her beloved grandfather, something that caught Valentina by surprise. One never knew another's heart.

Lola brought things back to the game. "Valentina, do they play much Mahjong in Italy?" "Oh no, but I do play, and I love it. I was sorry to miss out on joining the group earlier, but I had business concerns that were occupying so much of my time." She fibbed a little, but she did like Mahjong. Lola was keen to play the game of Mahjong, and whatever else sort of game might come of this new addition to their table. She had her suspicions about Doris and the secrets she had been keeping. Perhaps new things might be coming to light.

It seemed everyone at the Mahjong table had something in mind other than matching tiles. But match tiles they did, and at the end of the evening Valentina was not opposed to becoming a regular at the Mahjong table. Perhaps she needed more activities to fill her time rather than the precious minutes she had devoted to anticipating being with Jack.

Lola tried asking in every possible manner if there was any news of Doris's circumstances or family. Was there no one to take care of the details? The other three women were as clueless as she appeared to be. As the game progressed, Lola began to drop little bits of information about Doris, why she joined the dating website and her husband's unfortunate circumstance. Michelle and Valentina caught each other's eye periodically with a knowing expression, but neither of them ever let on that they had any new information.

Finally, the game concluded, and the women began to put things away and prepare to head out to their homes.

"Valentina, may I give you a lift?" Michelle asked, and Valentina wondered if she was as anxious to review the evening with her friend as she was.

They both said their goodbyes to Lola and Delta as they headed back through the store. "Wait just a minute, hon, I need some buttermilk for biscuits in the morning," she said, stopping at a display. Michelle liked being prepared for anything, including friends dropping by for breakfast. The promise of buttermilk biscuits made Valentina happy when Michelle suggested they should share the first meal of the day the next morning.

CHAPTER 10

Valentina woke up with a groan. The previous evening playing Mahjong was enough to make her back ache from sitting too long on the chairs at the Market Café. She had to admit, however, that the pain was worth it for the gossip she and Michelle had heard on the topic of Doris and her secret boyfriend.

Thinking of that made her remember that she was meeting her friend and John Watson in about forty-five minutes. She'd slept past her alarm, and now she was going to need to get in the shower before her first cup of coffee. She hoped that Michelle would have a big pot of coffee brewing at her house.

Valentina started to shed the oversized T-shirt she'd slept in, but before she could manage it the phone rang. She hesitated and considered calling the person back later, but instead reached for it and managed a cheery hello.

"Hi, beautiful." It was Jack.

"Good morning, I was just getting into the shower." That seemed to catch him off guard, as there was silence on the other end. Valentina instantly regretted how curt it sounded, as though she were brushing him off. "I just mean, you caught me just right. I would've missed you." "Oh, right. How are things there?"

Suddenly Valentina felt a slight ache where her pleasure at hearing Jack's voice should have been. "Fine. I do miss you, Jack. How are you?" Her voice was softened by the image of his face. "I miss you too. I, well, I just wanted to clear up anything you might have thought, umm... You know, about Yvonne. She wants me to help her with a new business venture, that's all. She really is trying to plan for her future, and the kids." He paused, leaving Valentina to mentally fill in the blanks. "Anyway, that's what I wanted to say to you. I need to get into the office this morning

but... Val, I do miss you. I'd like to see you this weekend, talk about some things." Talk? Valentina felt her stomach drop as she imagined what sort of conversation Jack had in mind. She was being silly. Just because a man wanted to talk didn't mean it was a bad thing. Scolding herself about it didn't help. "That sounds good. I can fix something nice for us and we'll just stay in and... talk." That word, *talk*, seemed like a doomsday threat. Even though Jack was

trying to downplay Yvonne having been in his apartment, something seemed off in the way he sounded, in what he was saying, and especially in how she felt.

"Okay, great. I'll be able to get down there by around noon, if that's good for you." Valentina did want to see Jack, but she dreaded the idea of him saying something she might not want to hear.

"Sounds perfect to me, see you then. *Ciao*." She waited for his reply with a lump in her throat she feared might choke her.

"Ha-ha, ciao, baby. See you Saturday."

Valentina chuckled at the familiar phrase; it was something Jack liked to say to her as though he were a suave continental type. She repeated it aloud, *ciao, baby*, as she stepped into the shower and turned the water on, letting it pour over her and wash away the tears she had been holding back.

After her shower, Valentina did a quick Nespresso cup of espresso, searching for a pair of tennis shoes while it brewed. She found the shoes and slipped them on, glad to have the opportunity to walk to Michelle's and enjoy the crisp fall air. Checking the clock on the kitchen wall, she took one last, rushed sip of coffee before heading out the door.

Just as she had hoped, the walk helped her to clear her mind a little, and now the idea of Jack's visit brought a smile to her face. Valentina had no reason to suspect that there was anything wrong, and as she walked, her mood brightened with each step. The leaves were beginning to change into brilliant shades of orange and yellow, with a few red spots visible in the woods beyond. With the colors of the season as inspiration, the menu for Saturday began to take shape in her head as she stepped up onto Michelle's front porch.

Michelle's house smelled like breakfast and autumn, with coffee and cinnamon wafting from her cheerful kitchen. John was already there when Valentina arrived. It was good to live close by, just a few minutes between their houses meant that Valentina and Michelle, and now John, could get together in a hurry, if need be. After the Mahjong and the gossip of the night before, the two women had plenty to tell John this morning.

"Hello!" Valentina said as she stepped in the kitchen, her mouth already beginning to water. Michelle was such a good cook, and this morning seemed like a fall day tailor made for a good Southern breakfast.

"Hi, sweetie, come on in." Michelle greeted her and produced a cup of coffee prepared just like Valentina liked it. John got up and offered a perfunctory bow, since he was the absolute embodiment of a proper Englishman. "Oh, this all smells so good! I woke up looking forward to coffee and anything you cook, although last night I was sure it would be buttermilk biscuits."

Valentina laughed along with Michelle as she shrugged and said, "The cinnamon simply won out!"

"So, have you told John any of the juicy bits we heard last night? Lola was certainly anxious to tell everything she knew." To be honest, Valentina had been surprised to hear the account of Doris's romance with a man from a dating service. Her husband was a long-term care patient, and yet she had advertised for another man to be with. And in perhaps a stroke of bad judgement, she had confided in Lola, who was now willing (and anxious) to tell anyone interested the details of a poor dead woman.

Michelle clucked her tongue in disapproval. "I hate that we were glad to hear it, but it will be helpful in our little investigation. At least now we know for certain that Doris used that dating service and met someone. The question is, did he kill her?"

Valentina nodded, still not sure about accusing him of murder. "He sounded very nice the way Lola described him, or at least the way Doris had. Lola never met him, did she? He seems to have had a business. Oh, that reminds me. The community board of directors has asked me to check into a security company to install some inexpensive equipment at our gate. They gave me a few leads that should help."

Michelle handed a plate to Valentina and then one to John. She had ladled on scrambled eggs and bacon, and some cinnamon crusted French toast topped with syrupy fried apples. "Eat up, y'all, we have some work to do."

"Oh, this looks good. *Buon appetito!*"

As the three friends enjoyed their breakfast, the discussion went back to Doris and the plan to test their theory that the killer was somewhere within the dating service John had used before moving to Long Lakes.

"I think that I should present myself as someone similar to these two women. Someone who is looking for some companionship on the side and I should have a husband who's either comatose or completely impaired."

John gave her a concerned look. "We mustn't be careless at any point, my dear. Wherever you go to meet anyone needs to be close by, if possible. Valentina and I must be present, I will not budge on that."

Michelle leaned across the bar to plant a kiss on John's cheek. "You are the dearest man, and I promise to not ever be out of your sight. Does that help?"

Valentina thought she saw a slight blush in the older man's complexion. John simply smiled back at Michelle.

From Michelle's back porch, a demanding *mroww* sounded. "Oh dear, I think Sherlock has had quite enough of the great outdoors." John got up from his seat and went to open the screen door. His beautiful black cat came sauntering inside and flopped down on the rug in front of a small settee. Following him was Michelle's cat, Mina. The two had a mutual agreement to co exist when circumstances demanded it of the affable felines. Mina wandered into the kitchen and meowed her request for a treat of some sort from Michelle. It was an impossibility to overindulge a cat, no matter her breeding.

Valentina took the last bite of her French toast as she watched the cats, making a mental note to add dog treats to her market list. "Michelle, I am so full that I might, as you say it, pop!" Valentina patted her stomach. She was glad she would be walking back home after this meal because she would need the exercise to undo the calories. "So, what about this dating profile of yours? We need to make it sound good, but of course that means we need to be good liars." Valentina winked at her co-conspirators. If Jack ever got wind of this plan he'd put a stop to it, of that she was certain.

Michelle cleared away the empty plates and rinsed them before placing them in the dishwasher. "Let's all go into the living room and get on with it. Valentina sweetheart, did you bring your laptop?"

As she arose from the table Valentina nodded. "Yes, I left it in there. Perhaps we should go down to the market when we upload it. I don't want anyone able to trace it back to your house." She noticed that both Michelle and John looked surprised. Of course, they hadn't thought of that. She was a little more computer literate than her friends, but at times like this she wished her daughter, Bea, was close by and able to help.

The profile had to be fashioned to resemble those of the two dead women. If their theory was correct, and they agreed it was at least probable, then Michelle needed to convey the same information. Luckily, the profile for Doris was still online, a serious oversight on the part of whoever kept tabs on people. For the trio of sleuths, it was a fortunate break. "Doris's profile states that she was looking for companionship only, nothing long term. I can do that. And we know from the obituary that John found on Marilyn Durbin that her husband is in convalescent care, so we can assume she wanted something similar to what Doris posted." Michelle was sitting close to Valentina so she could read what was on the screen. As she scrolled through the list of choices, Michelle would reply yes or no to how it should be answered. Multiple choice certainly made it easier, but they needed to find the spot where the condition of the husbands was described.

"Oh, I see it. Comments can be added at the end to tell why people choose to sign up. Doris's says that she is lonely without her husband able to live with her, and that she loves him but knows he would want her to have good company during these difficult days. Oh my, that is well said. I wonder if it was true."

Valentina was wary of these types of websites but knowing that a woman could try to replace her husband so easily was difficult for her to understand. Perhaps that was the reason for the killer's act, a type of retribution for being unfaithful. "I think I know why these women were killed."

Michelle's eyes widened. "You do? That was quick, what gives it away?"

Valentina looked at John and Michelle, thinking she might have spoken too soon. But the reasoning was sound. "These women were cheating on their husbands, right out in the open. A man might be tempted to punish such a woman, especially if he's been through something similar. What do you think?"

Michelle looked at John and he returned a puzzled expression as she spoke. "I think it makes perfect sense. These women are advertising for a gigolo while admitting that their husbands are ill or confined to a hospital. They aren't widows; they're just bored and lonely."

John looked slightly uncomfortable when Michelle used the word gigolo. "I certainly would not have chosen to date women who had husbands, no matter the circumstance. Valentina, you may be right about this fellow; he's defending the honor of these men whether they know it or not."

Michelle started to giggle. "My dear, I would never mistake you for a gigolo. But then maybe that wasn't the intention these women had. Maybe they only wanted someone to accompany them to a movie or a concert, or any number of places where a woman feels uncomfortable being alone in a crowd. You would have been a perfect gentleman, Mister Watson, I have no doubt."

Continuing with the profile, Michelle and Valentina read through their work and, agreeing it was a job well done, called it finished. Now, all that was needed was to upload it to the website and wait for responses. Having taken on the technical responsibilities, it was up to Valentina to get this part of the scheme in motion.

"Give me a username and a password, and I will be set." Valentina would add this to the items on her list of things to do.

Michelle made a face at the task of a password then jotted down her idea. "What do you think about this one? *IDRWAD68.*"

Valentina looked at the paper and then back at Michelle. "What does it mean?" Michelle rolled her eyes, answering with a smirk. "It means *'I don't really want a date'*, and the number is the year I was born."

That made Valentina laugh, but it also revealed to her that Michelle might be having some second thoughts about their plan.

"Of course you want a date! That's the point, Michelle, to get you a date. Only you won't go alone, John and I will be with you all the way." She reached out and gave her friend a hug. It was very brave of Michelle to take this on, so the job was to keep her safe. Valentina turned to John and let him see the computer screen. "Here, John, take a look at this and see what you think."

The Englishman sat down next to Valentina and read through the profile, nodding at times and frowning slightly at others.

"Well done, darling. You sound irresistible." He kissed Michelle and squeezed her hand. "Oh, that reminds me, we need a picture of you in something slightly provocative." Valentina knew that her friend must certainly have an outfit that was suitable for trying to entice a suitor. Michelle got up and walked to the bedroom, emerging a few minutes later wearing a blue lace dress. Her hair was slightly rumpled looking, but in a way that made her look like she'd come in off the beach, tousled but pretty and feminine. John whistled and Michelle blushed. "Oh, that is perfect. Here, let me get your picture out on the porch, something natural." The women went outside onto the porch and laughed about their scheme, wondering aloud if it would work. In the wake of possible danger, the two of them found something amusing in playing the game. Perhaps it was more a type of nervousness, because considering what or who they might encounter this could become more like *The Hunger Games* than an evening playing *CLUE*.

With the photo on her phone and the phony profile on her laptop, Valentina felt as though the plan was ready to be launched. Michelle and John were resolute about doing this, and Valentina wouldn't want them to go alone on this journey. She wondered again whether they should include Jack in their investigation of Doris's death, but she decided not to say anything unless the others agreed to it.

Michelle went back to her bedroom to change out of the dress and back into her jeans and T-shirt. John put Sherlock in his blue harness as he prepared for the walk home, explaining that there were tasks waiting for him there. Valentina observed the tenderness between John and Michelle as he gave her a kiss while she placed both of her hands on his face, framing him as though he were a portrait she needed to remember. Valentina's breath caught at the sight of it, recognizing her own yearning to be with Jack.

Valentina decided to walk back to her house and get the bicycle for her trip into the marketplace. The town site had grown since she first moved to Long Lakes, and the basket she had on her bicycle would allow for the few items she wanted to pick up there. She said her goodbyes to John and Michelle, letting them have some privacy. Tasks or not, John didn't really seem to be in a hurry to leave his lady love.

The sun was warm on Valentina's skin as she walked, the early morning frost no longer visible. Her thoughts went to the journey on which she was embarking with Michelle and John. Somewhere, a killer was reviewing his work and possibly planning to strike again. Would they encounter him? Was this something they would all regret?

Valentina hoped for safety and wisdom in all of it, but she wasn't sure of either.

CHAPTER 11

When Valentina reached her house, the phone in her jacket pocket started to ring. She sat down on the porch, pulled it out and pushed the green button. It was one of her accounts in Nashville, and the storeowner was keen to have a meeting with her and the distributor as soon as she could make the drive. Since it was still early enough, Valentina offered to meet them at around three o'clock. She could spend the night in the city and head back home tomorrow. Perhaps Jack would have time to join her for dinner and start the weekend early.

After the details with the storeowner were worked out, Valentina went inside and grabbed a bottle of water from the fridge before heading into the bedroom to pack an overnight bag. First, she needed to change clothes, since her leggings and T-shirt wouldn't do for a business meeting.

Dressed in a pair of tan linen trousers and a white Charmeuse sleeveless blouse, Valentina looked the picture of cool. She slipped on a pair of black flats that would also go with the pair of jeans in her overnight bag. Pulling a brush through her hair helped to calm down the effects of some light humidity, and then the finishing touch: a pair of black obsidian earrings given to her by her daughter, Bea. They had been a gift after the divorce, a sort of protection against negativity and other unpleasantness. Neither she nor Bea believed in such things, and yet Valentina tended to wear the earrings when going into meetings or stressful situations. Perhaps she did believe the stones possessed some special powers, or hoped they did.

Valentina took a lightweight jacket from her hall closet and made a final check of the house and the dog dishes, making sure there was plenty of food and water for them. The recently installed doggie door ensured they could go in and out at will, and she trusted them to be good guard dogs while she was gone.

As she closed the door behind her, with purse and brief-case in hand, she went over a mental checklist of every-thing, including the thumb drive with Michelle's profile for the dating site. Getting farther away from Long Lakes was probably a very good idea as far as the IP address was concerned. All in all, the meeting in Nashville was turning out to be a good thing.

It was a beautiful day, and the two and a half hours' drive would be a nice way to spend it. She always dreaded the traffic in Nashville, but it was a fun city and the store she was visiting had

a nice location. Valentina decided to get in a little window shopping, since with the change in the seasons she would enjoy finding a few new things for the house.

It always surprised Valentina to come upon the city so suddenly. The countryside seemed to disappear behind her, giving way to the inevitable freeway gridlock. With the help of her GPS she started looking for the I-65 signs and made her way into the merging traffic that would take her to the destination. The voice began calling out instructions that Valentina followed carefully, merging onto the White Bridge Pike and then making a series of right turns. Within a few minutes, she was at her destination and caught sight of the little gourmet shop that carried her wines.

She saw Greg Greeson's BMW Z4 and pulled in next to it. Her truck looked like a giant next to the little roadster, but it fit in nicely with so many other trucks. The fun of Nashville was that you never knew who might be driving one of those shiny new trucks, and the possibility of running into one of the many recording artists that called

Nashville home was real. Her distributor was waiting on the sidewalk in front of the store, briefcase in hand. Valentina opened her door as he came alongside, offering his hand to her as she stepped onto the running board and down to the pavement.

"Hello, Greg. Thank you for meeting me here on such short notice." Valentina really liked Greg and appreciated how willing he had been to help her learn the ropes of the business she had started when she moved to America. As a distributor, Greg Greeson was required to attend these meetings between the storeowner and the supplier, but he never said no to Valentina.

"Valentina," Greg reached out and gave her a quick hug. "I'm always at your service. And Vincent is a great guy; I think we're both grateful to be doing business with him." Valentina nodded in agreement, adding that she valued them both.

Greg took Valentina's elbow as they stepped up onto the walkway in front of the store. The other spaces in this little mall were all taken except for one, three doors down from Vincent's Gourmet. The name said it all, and business always seemed brisk despite being close to a Trader Joe's store just around the corner. They seemed to co-exist peacefully in this location.

Valentina turned to her right at the sound of a woman's voice. It sounded as though the woman had called someone Jack, and when the reply came from a man getting out of a Jeep, it was with shock that she realized the two voices belonged to Yvonne and Jack.

Her Jack.

There was no time to investigate the situation as Vincent was at the door to his store, welcoming her and Greg. She would see about Jack and Yvonne after this meeting, although she wondered if she really wanted to know more. Jack had said something about a new business venture for his ex-wife. Perhaps it was a store of some sort. Still, why involve Jack?

Walking inside the store had a calming effect on Valentina. Vincent was an artist, and he had created such a beautiful environment, with food and the wine arranged by region and then by pairings. He had done all the work necessary for his clients to choose the items one might need for a party or a relaxing afternoon. Valentina saw one of her labels situated among a selection of hard cheeses and cold cuts. It was a Morellino produced by a small boutique winery in Scansano. Of course, Vincent had placed it perfectly with the cold cuts.

"Vincent, the store looks beautiful. I never get tired of coming in here." Valentina meant it sincerely. "So tell us, what can we do for you today?"

Vincent launched into his ideas about how to grow his business and the plans he was considering about expansion. The question was whether Valentina, his favorite vendor, could meet the demands of an even larger market. Greg raised his eyebrows, but this store was on the rise and expanding might be a perfect move to make at this moment. Valentina took a deep breath, appreciating the offer to be Vincent's primary importer and what it might mean for her as a businesswoman. She caught a look from Greg and immediately began to consider what it would be like to take on a partner. Greg was perfect for the job.

Valentina knew it was a decision to be made after some careful examination of her books and her resources. She would be placing a lot of eggs in someone else's basket. And what about a partner? She wasn't certain about inviting someone else into her little business, but if she needed to do that, it was Greg who could manage it without getting in her way.

She let her mind drift back to seeing Yvonne and Jack earlier and knew that it was a situation she needed to face head on.

"Vincent, can you give me a few days to think about this? I love your ideas and the prospect of being involved is tempting. I must look at my records and my suppliers. You understand."

Valentina wouldn't lead him to believe anything she couldn't be certain would work. His expression told her she was doing it the right way.

"Of course, Valentina, I'm not rushing into this either. I want a team of good people who are committed to building a business that will be around for a long time. You take your time, and Greg..." Vincent held out his hand and the two men shook on the merits of this presentation. "You have a place in this depending on what you and Valentina work out. I have a meeting with the owner of this center in two weeks. He's on vacation right now. Let's see if we can meet again before then, maybe you'll have reached some decisions."

The three of them agreed to another meeting in ten days, which would be enough time to give it serious thought and check on things that were needful. Valentina looked around the store again. It was so pretty and inviting. She had no doubts that Vincent would make another location an even better place. Looking at a large advertising poster that featured the Tuscan countryside suddenly made Valentina a little homesick for Italy. There were days when she missed it, and the life it used to be for her and her family. But those days were gone, and she couldn't get them back. She couldn't even be sure of keeping what had been gained here, and her thoughts went back to seeing Yvonne and Jack getting out of their cars. She wondered if they were still there and decided to walk down to that empty storefront.

Greg and Valentina said their goodbyes to Vincent and

walked out of the store into a brisk fall afternoon. "Say, do you have plans for dinner tonight?"

It wouldn't be the first time they'd shared a meal, but Valentina had other things on her mind. She knew that Greg had a crush on her, but she needed to investigate what she hoped wasn't happening between Jack and Yvonne. Her plan to have dinner with Jack no longer seemed like a good idea.

"Can I call you later about that? I might need to check in with one more thing while I'm in Nashville." It wasn't a lie, she just didn't need to elaborate about what she intended to do. If she was honest with herself, Valentina wasn't certain she wanted to be with Jack right now. This situation with Yvonne was a problem for her, and unless Jack had a good reason for being with his ex-wife, it presented a change for their relationship.

Greg seemed more than happy to wait to hear from Valentina. While he pulled out of his parking space and headed into traffic, Valentina noticed that Jack's and Yvonne's cars were still in front of the empty store. She decided to walk down to it and see what was going on. The days were getting shorter and at four-thirty in the afternoon, the sun was nearly done with its day. All of the streetlights were on, and the shop windows now had brightly lit interiors to show off the products inside. Valentina approached the shop where she knew she'd find

Jack and was surprised when the door opened, and Yvonne walked out.

Both women stopped in their tracks and took in the other with an appraising eye. Yvonne had on jeans and a light blue turtleneck. Her blonde hair spilled over her shoulders making her seem more youthful than she was. It irritated Valentina, and suddenly she felt a wave of insecurity wash over her. Yvonne was a pretty woman, and in the brief seconds it took for this encounter, Valentina felt defeated and lonely. Jack was next out the door, accompanied by an older fellow who was probably the real estate agent. This must've been the store Jack had mentioned for Yvonne's new business.

"Valentina!" Jack immediately stepped towards her and embraced her, quickly—almost too quickly—then letting her go.

"*Ciao, ciao...* such a surprise to see you here." Valentina said, smiling. Though she knew instinctively that there were maneuverings going on, and that Jack was like most men in his inability to understand how women worked. "I had a meeting with one of my customers who is considering expanding his business. I thought I would walk down here and see about this unit." Valentina noticed the expression on the agent's face seemed a little brighter; he might have a bidding war on his hands.

Valentina expected some sort of reply now, but no one spoke for a good ten seconds. After that awkward pause, Jack said, "Yvonne and I are going to take the kids out for pizza, if you'd like to join us."

Valentina thought Yvonne was going to strangle Jack for asking her to join them. She almost laughed out loud but decided against it. "Thank you, but I have a dinner engagement with my distributor. We have details to discuss." Then, before she could stop herself, she added, "You

remember Greg Greeson, don't you, Jack? He's been so helpful and will be involved in this expansion for Vincent's business."

Valentina knew that Jack had been a little jealous of Greg at one point, and therefore didn't feel the slightest bit guilty about rubbing his nose in it now. But Yvonne looked pleased, and Jack frowned as if he thought better of her, which made Valentina regret having mentioned Greg. It didn't matter. She would go to dinner with Greg and let Jack and Yvonne parent their children.

Jack did look a little disappointed, but wasn't this what he had tried to have the courage to accomplish? Valentina thought she saw something else in his eyes, a sadness that didn't belong there if he was with someone he wanted in his life. Could she have it all wrong?

"Well, I'd better get going. I'm staying at the Opryland Hotel. I have several complimentary nights there from Greg's company."

"Oh," he said, and Valentina wondered why she was trying so hard. *She* was Jack's girlfriend. Even if Yvonne were standing there ready to have a family night, he was her *ex-husband* and had no hold on him. Valentina, on the other hand, was Jack's girlfriend and he was coming to stay with her this weekend.

"*Ci vediamo sabato, amore.*" Valentina kissed him gently and let her right hand touch his face before backing away. Jack knew what she had said but she doubted that Yvonne could translate it, except perhaps the *amore*. A sudden sense of satisfaction came over Valentina as she waved goodbye and headed back to her truck. It was all she could do to get up into the truck without jumping, but she managed to make it smooth. She wished briefly that she had been driving Greg's little roadster, but the biggest part of her departure had been successful.

Yvonne might have Jack for that evening's family outing, but come the weekend he was all hers. Valentina would enjoy her evening with Greg, download Michelle's phony profile to the dating website, and then sleep with the satisfaction of having stood up for herself and for Jack. What a day! Valentina had to wonder what the rest of this week would bring.

CHAPTER 12

The agenda for murder is a daunting thing, and at times malleable in the mind of a killer. What seemed like a perfect formula for retribution on behalf of the wounded slowly becomes a matter of personal satisfaction. What starts out as a cause becomes a vendetta that eliminates the worst offenders, the betrayers. And what is betrayal without a villain, or villainess?

An overheard conversation between two friends might be the catalyst for a new chapter in this vendetta. Two people sharing their plans for cheating on their spouses, the admission of guilt by one who had betrayed his or her spouse and broken the seal of sanctity that should have accompanied their vows to remain faithful and trustworthy.

A conversation such as that might spur the self-righteous to act. It might be a reason to kill. The two women whose conversation he had been eavesdropping on paid their bill and got up to leave the restaurant. A slow burn was building up as the killer watched them approach the valet stand. He knew this was a deviation from how he had designed his plan for punishing those who betrayed their spouses and was not within the parameters he had designed. But wasn't cheating on a spouse his criteria? Not just those whose husbands were helpless or trapped inside crippled bodies. He needed to teach a lesson to those whose actions demanded punishment. He left money on the table and got up to follow the women, a blonde and a redhead. The blonde was tall and lanky, athletic he thought. The redhead was stunning, a woman who would have had no difficulty in finding a new lover, perhaps more than one. He hoped that she would be last so that he could describe how her friend faced death and judgment. Not having used the valet made it possible to get to his car quickly and watch them. He was formulating a plan, perhaps not his best and certainly not following his usual method, but he knew what he would do when the time arrived. The women were traveling together in a new Saab convertible. It was not a common car, but it did speak of a degree of ego if not affluence. The redhead was driving with the top down on this beautiful autumn day, and the sun glinted off the auburn hair in such a way that it seemed probable the color wasn't natural. In many relationships between women there was one who was much more attractive than her friend. The

gifted or beautiful seemed to always have people around them who were less so, as though they needed to outshine someone close to them.

The observation was fleeting, and his thoughts returned to the task at hand. He assumed that the blonde would be dropped off at her house and the redhead would go home. He would need to follow her, find out where she lived and then go back for the other one; they had each admitted to cheating and so he was obligated to punish both of them. He was like the angel of death, the dispenser of justice to the unjust. His calling was a holy thing; he had no remorse for doing the work of a vengeful god, even if it were a god of his own design and invention.

One had to have patience to travel through the newly renovated Knoxville downtown. Once clear of the many bustling new restaurants and shops of the district, the car moved towards the suburbs. The homes were nice, a mixture of new builds on old lots and the venerable old homes that had withstood time and weather. That the redhead was driving caused a sort of thrill for the killer, his choice was not his choice at all; this was destiny.

The Saab pulled up in front of an older house, and after some goodbyes, the blonde got out and headed to a porch decorated with hanging pots of flowers and rattan furniture. Instead of going directly inside, she climbed the steps and sat down on the rattan settee, pulled out her phone and made a call. The killer wished he could hear the conversation and presumed the call was to her lover.

It would be the last time she dialed that number.

He followed as the Saab continued on past the tree-lined street, turning right at a four-way stop and then right again to pull into the driveway of an elegant new home between two old craftsman style bungalows. Her house was a modern farmhouse, painted white with a wrap around porch that featured hanging ferns between every post. It seemed out of place in this setting, more for show than substance. Unlike her friend, the redhead opened her front door and was nearly knocked down by two young children who wrapped their arms around their mother's legs, laughing with her as she kissed each of them on the tops of their heads.

No. This wouldn't work. He couldn't kill a woman with her children in the house. His fists clenched. He didn't have a plan, and so he would fail. Damn it, why had he tried to change the

plan? As the redhead closed the door behind her, she reached inside a pocket and withdrew her phone.

He sat there, wondering if he should go back to the blonde woman's house. But no. This was a sign. An avenging angel need never veer from his assignment. He had a plan and needed to stick to it. The two women had been saved by those two children; perhaps they would repent of their sin and avoid some other avenging angel. Somewhere from the depths of his soul, he hoped that was true.

He pulled away from the curb and continued on, leaving the neighborhood behind him in search of a worthy victim. Downtown Knoxville had changed over the years of civic improvements and refurbishing old buildings. His office was a two-story rental in an old industrial building that had been redesigned as lofts. The downstairs was a showroom and design space, and his upstairs was office and home. He had three employees, two designers and a salesman. They all liked to refer to the workspace as the "war room", as though what they did here constituted some great visionary thing. It had a degree of ingenuity, but in the end it was all about feeding the human need for distraction and amusement while assuming a sense of privacy.

He sat down at his desk, perusing the profiles of several women who seemed to fit into the category from which he culled his victims. He shuddered at his near miss earlier, the temptation to step outside of the parameters of his search. What he had learned from his own encounter with betrayal was that anyone could be lured into murdering another person. His wife had attempted to have him killed but had instead met her own death. What that began for him was a journey fraught with despair and, eventually, the satisfaction of saving people from a worse fate. The husbands whose wives were now no longer a threat to them might recover, just as he had.

As he read through profiles, one person caught his eye, and she seemed to be exactly what he detested. This woman admitted to being married to a man who was not expected to recover from a debilitating stroke, and her desire was to have a companion to soothe her loneliness. She was attractive for her age, and had a wide range of interests. She loved museums and going to concerts; she would even consider traveling with an appropriate companion rather than having

to go alone. He wondered what she might expect and how she would arrange their accommodations.

With one click, a new chapter was opened. Musing to himself, he typed a message to her. "Michelle, it's so nice to meet you. My name is..."

CHAPTER 13

Friday morning came along quickly. The days spent watching for a reply from a possible murderer had consumed a great deal of imagination and anticipation on the part of the three conspirators. As requested by Long Lakes' HOA, Valentina had contacted a security expert to put things right at the front gate to the community, and her preparations for the weekend with Jack were all neatly aligned.

It was all a little crazy.

Valentina's French press was snuggled in a dish towel as the coffee did a slow brew. She had added a pinch of cinnamon and two drops of vanilla to complement a beautiful autumn morning; the change of season made her yearn for a cozy fire and Jack by her side.

"Tomorrow, that's not so long to wait," she said, but scolded herself. She had decided long ago that it was not a sign of insanity to have a conversation with herself... out loud. The dogs were good listeners, but they never actually had any good advice for her musings.

As Valentina poured her coffee into a cup from a local artisan's pottery shop, the aroma inspired her. If she were a writer she might have composed something beautiful to commemorate it.

The first sip was interrupted by the sound of her phone. Debating whether to answer it, Valentina gave in to the inevitable curiosity. It might be important. "Buongiorno." "Well, *bonjorno* to you too, sweetie." It was Michelle, and her attempt at Italian was awful. Valentina had to laugh at the effort.

"Guess what? I have a date!"

Valentina's jaw dropped. That wasn't just any date. It was *a date with someone from the website*. Michelle had been receiving inquiries since her profile went up, but so far, she hadn't followed up on any of them. None of them had seemed like the right fellow. That this one had passed muster with Michelle was exciting, to say the least.

According to Michelle, the man in question was slightly arrogant, a characteristic that seemed to spark a real curiosity in the newly in-demand Michelle. Valentina felt a strange mixture of excitement and dread as she anticipated what was now a real plan put in action.

"What do you think, is he suspicious enough for you?" Michelle asked.

"Could be. When is the date happening?"

As Michelle began to give the details, Valentina interrupted her. "I have coffee and biscotti, why don't you come over and we can talk about this?"

Michelle agreed, it was always better in person. Valentina opened a tin of almond biscotti that she had baked using her mother's recipe. It was one of the ways that Valentina kept her homeland close, the tastes and aromas of Italy.

It only took Michelle ten minutes to get to Valentina's front door, choosing to ride her bike rather than walk. Hugs and smiles only hinted at the excitement brewing. Michelle started her account of what had transpired since yesterday while Valentina filled her mug with coffee and lifted the lid to the tin of biscotti. Michelle took a cookie as she reiterated the decision to only open the emails while she was at the Market, still concerned about revealing where she lived.

"I went down to the bakery and had a cup of coffee there and checked the email account we set up. I saw there was a notification, a little smiley face from a fella named Sam Albertson. He's a—"

Valentina stopped her, a strange expression on her face. "His name is Sam Albertson? Does he have a security business?"

Michelle's jaw dropped as she dipped her biscotti into the steaming coffee. "How on earth did you know that? I haven't even told John yet."

Valentina just shook her head at this very odd coincidence. Or was it? "The security guy I talked to about security at our front gate, his name is Sam Albertson. I'm supposed to meet him tomorrow morning. I hate taking time away from Jack but he said it was the only time he could get out here. Michelle, what are the chances that he also contacted you?"

Michelle bit into her soggy cookie, then took a sip of coffee. "Are we crazy? I mean, well I don't know what I mean. I want to do this but the same fella showin' up twice, that's weird." Valentina had to agree, but it piqued her interest in the man in a way that required some answers. "When is your date, and where? Jack is coming in this weekend and if we need to keep our eyes on you, I might have to tell him what we're doing."

"I'm meeting him in Dewey, at that cute little diner. I didn't want to drive too far, so I just told him that I live in the country, about halfway for each of us. We're supposed to do this tomorrow for a late lunch." Michelle's mouth dropped open. "A late lunch because he has a business appointment in the morning. Oh my *gawd*, it must be the same man!"

The two women were silent for a few minutes, sipping coffee and dunking biscotti until this odd scenario began to take shape in their minds. Valentina was seriously considering telling Jack about all of it, the entire plan. If this man, Sam Albertson, was the killer, he was returning to the scene of the crime and possibly creating a way to have access to Long Lakes with whatever he installed as a security measure. There had been precautions taken to hide Michelle's location, but this guy was a tech guy. It was possible he'd caught on to their ruse.

"What if I change the location, move it here?' Michelle looked at her friend for an answer. Valentina nodded, dislodging a wisp of hair that reminded her she needed to make an appointment for a trim. That wasn't too bad, and it would be easier to keep tabs on her and perhaps not require telling Jack, at least not now. "It would be a lot easier, and you can make the excuse that you're invited to dinner by a resident."

Valentina's phone rang; the name that came up made her gasp. Michelle took note of it as she took another sip of coffee. She got up and went to the back porch to give Valentina some privacy. With a shuddering breath, Valentina answered. "Hello?"

"Hello, this is Sam with the security company, confirming our ten tomorrow?" Valentina needed to make a quick decision about this Sam Albertson fellow. If there were any chance at all that he was the man they were after, there was no way she could give him access to Long Lakes. She had to think fast as the scenario wound around her imagination. "I am so sorry, Mister Albertson, to be so late informing you but, uh... well, the contract was awarded to another company that already does business with one of the other communities. It is merely a matter of familiarity, you understand. We will pay you for any time you have already billed to our account." She heard a deep sigh from the other end, making her wonder if she'd just put a man out of work on a crazy hunch.

"I understand, it's not personal... it's business." Sam's reply had a cold edge to it.

Valentina had to consider if she was risking reprisals of some sort. "Thank you so much for understanding. This is something that was out of my control, unfortunately. Good luck, Mister Albertson."

She ended the call and went out to the back porch. She'd barely closed the screen door behind her when Michelle asked, "What did Mr. Albertson want?"

"He wanted to confirm our meeting tomorrow morning, but I told him that we gave the contract to another company." Valentina caught sight of the squirrels, which made her think of nuts. She was wondering if maybe she and Michelle, and John, were just a little bit nutty as well.

Michelle looked surprised, but understood the reasoning. "So, you lied to him?" She clucked her tongue in mock disapproval, smiling as she did so.

"Here, let me have your cup and I'll freshen up your coffee."

Valentina stopped in her tracks and turned back around to face Michelle. "You need to call Sam and tell him you've had an invitation to stay with your friend for the weekend. Ask if he can meet you here, and I will be your friend."

Michelle giggled at that. "But you are my friend, or did you forget?"

Valentina turned back to the kitchen and poured fresh coffee. "If you're visiting someone here then you don't have to worry about him tracking you because you're telling him where you are, and that it's just a visit. If lunch goes well perhaps you should invite him to dinner at my house."

Michelle took in a deep breath before a sip of coffee. "So, we are setting a trap?" Valentina smiled and shook her head. "No, it's more of a test. I want to see if he can tell a story that we believe. Okay, maybe it's a trap."

The two friends raised their cups in a toast to a plan in motion and their hope for success. "Don't give him my name tomorrow, just see if he takes the bait and comes to dinner at my house and we'll surprise him. I want to see his reaction to us knowing each other." Michelle nodded, but her expression held concern. "What if he already knows? If he's such a techy hot shot, then he might have already figured it out. He's starting to seem like a scary-ass dude, to paraphrase a line from *Friends*."

Valentina stared, confused. "What friend said that? I don't understand."

Michelle laughed. "Not a friend, the TV show *Friends*. It's something that Chandler says, about a scary-ass clown." She rolled her eyes at the blank look on Valentina's face. "Oh well, I guess you had to be there. Anyway, I feel better about staying closer to home. But he's going to know where you live."

Just then the doorbell rang. Valentina got up to answer the door and was greeted by a delivery girl from the new florist at the Market Square. She was surprised, assuming it was from Jack but not expecting something like this from him. She reached into the drawer of an entry table where she kept a small amount of cash and pulled out a five-dollar bill. Thanking the girl, Valentina closed the door and looked for a card.

"What's going on out... Oh my, look at those flowers!" Michelle said, clearly impressed by the beautiful and extravagant bouquet. "Jack has outdone himself; those are gorgeous." Valentina agreed, the flowers were beautiful, but they weren't from Jack. Once again, it was a bizarre situation and at the center of it was Sam Albertson. "Can you believe he's sending me flowers and he has a date with you tomorrow? I don't know if this guy is dangerous or stupid. Maybe he is both. That makes him doubly dangerous, I suppose."

"What does it say? Is it romantic or business? Although, that doesn't look like a business bouquet."

Valentina read the card out loud, "Thank you for the opportunity to serve your community. I'm looking forward to seeing you in person, and hope that these flowers will keep you smiling. Regards, Sam." Valentina thought back to her offer to pay any expenses that Sam would have billed to Long Lakes. These flowers would probably be on that bill.

"Okay, so he's making a point by sending flowers. Still, him being in contact with both of us is bizarre."

Valentina agreed, and now she thought that telling Jack was a good idea and would provide a measure of peace of mind. She was amazed that the first time out they had a candidate for the bad guy.

Michelle needed to head out. She had things to get done today including dropping in on John Watson. Valentina watched her friend pedal off towards her gentleman friend's house, and then began the various tasks she needed to finish today. Jack would be there soon, and she still had housework and cooking on her list.

The day flew by, just like the week that was winding down. Valentina had been working on some light cleaning, laundering sheets and towels, and prepping for the meal she'd serve tonight. Now she had just enough time to get into the shower before Jack arrived. He had said around five o'clock the last time they talked. He had a habit of changing times, mostly due to his work, or traffic. Either way, she wanted to get in the shower and be ready when he arrived.

It seemed like a pre-arranged inconvenience that the phone often started to ring just as she was stepping into the shower. She looked at the display and shivered.

It was Sam Albertson. Why was he calling? Their meeting was cancelled. It made her feel uncomfortable and she imagined that he was close by, watching her.

"Oh, hello, Mister Albertson," she said, once again, trying to keep her voice calm. "Hello, I was checking to see if you received the flowers?"

"Oh, yes, they were lovely. You are kind to have sent them, I'll let the community board of directors know how, ummm... you obviously care about your clients. Again, my apologies for the change."

"You're welcome. No hard feelings but I do have a small bill to submit. I realized that I don't have your address so I can mail it to you."

An alarm sounded in Valentina's head. "I think you should submit it to the email address, the same one to which you sent your resume. Yes, that will do just fine. Thank you again for the flowers and my apologies as I need to cut our conversation short. *Ciao*, good night." Her heart was racing from the conversation and the doorbell was ringing. What was it about trying to take a shower that always set off alarms and bells ringing? Valentina needed to put on a robe and go answer the door; another interruption while she tried to get ready for Jack.

She ran down the stairs and was nearly breathless when she opened the door. Jack looked at Valentina and then gave her a big smile as he walked into the house. Wasting no time, he scooped her up into his arms and kissed her as he carried her upstairs.

CHAPTER 14

Sherlock was a natural sleuth and living with a proper English gentleman like John Watson had served the black feline well during their tenure as friends and companions. As his human huddled next to the female he had taken to spending time with, the images on the screen were not lost to the intelligent cat. He watched as figures appeared and disappeared on the computer screen, not seeming to be concerned about any of it but carefully scrutinizing everything that his golden hued eyes observed. Being a cat, Sherlock embodied the particular wisdom and instincts of his species, and when one image in particular showed up on the screen he mewed seductively and touched it with one velvety paw.

"What? Sherlock my man, do you have an opinion about all of this?" John Watson respected his cat's feline inclinations and suggested to Michelle that she scroll back to the photograph indicated by Sherlock's paw. Michelle obliged and then read aloud the profile information on this most recent 'invitation' to form a connection, as the website phrased it.

"*Athletic and in love with the great outdoors, I love to explore new restaurants and experience new things. In my professional life I am an entrepreneur in the emerging field of... well, that's for you to find out.*" John raised an eyebrow at that. "Cheeky fellow, perhaps Sherlock is onto something."

Michelle smiled at her beau, as she preferred to call him, and continued reading. "*My home is in Knoxville, Tennessee, just a short drive from the beautiful Smoky Mountains. I would love to show you my neck of the woods. I am looking for a woman who will be loyal and loving, not necessarily a life partner but willing to be swept up into an adventurous new lifestyle with a man who is romantic and indulgent with both his finances and his heart.*" Michelle let a sigh escape her lips.

Sherlock observed all of this, listening to the sounds of human conversation and depending on his excellent cattish sense of interpretation. Something intrigued his humans about this image on their... to be honest he didn't know what it was. However, he had sussed out something to which they were now responding. He lay down with his head on the computer keyboard and waited while John and Michelle discussed what she had read.

149

THE END

ACKNOWLEDGMENTS

I would like to thank my invaluable collaborators, Glenna Meredith, Cyn Balog and Jayne Lewis, who contributed with their skills to turn my jumbled ideas into an actual book.

But, as usual, the person I would like to thank most is you, my esteemed Reader. Without you my books would be meaningless. I hope you enjoyed Valentina's adventures, and that you will continue to stick with us!

Last but not least, my thanks to my loving and talented daughter, Costanza, who will soon bloom as an author herself. I look forward to reading your next books!

ABOUT THE AUTHOR

Antonella L.M. Rivalta is a full-time translator and localization specialist but, as soon as she clocks out of her day job, she shifts gears and writes gripping romantic suspense novels.

Born and raised in Milano, Italy, three years ago Antonella decided to take the leap from Italy to the United States, along with her perplexed husband, culture-shocked daughter, two stoic dogs and a very sullen cat. After settling in a beautiful gated community in the Tennessee woods, she immediately decided to follow her heart's pull and start writing the action-packed thriller novels that slowly but steadily take shape in her head during her long hikes. Her own experiences in adjusting to such a vastly different culture are a constant source of inspiration for the Long Lakes series' main character, Valentina.

When she is not burning the midnight oil writing her next novel, Antonella spends her free time reading, looking for hard-to-find ingredients for her Italian dishes, walking her two Collies and traveling the USA in her RV. An outdoor enthusiast, she enjoys mountain biking and hiking in the Smokies.

For more information about Antonella and her books, visit www.antonellarivalta.com

BOOKS BY THIS AUTHOR

The Long Lakes Thrillers

Elsewhere

Behind the gates lies a secluded community with secrets to die for . . .

The idyllic gated community of Long Lakes, Tennessee, is the perfect location for Italian-born Valentina Bianco to start over after her painful divorce. Except the town isn't the quiet refuge she thinks it is.

Undercover FBI agent Jack Erikson doesn't know what to make of the fiery, outspoken beauty he encounters at the general store. He can't afford to get on the wrong side of the locals while he's investigating a suspected fraud and is determined to win Valentina over.

Valentina can't deny the spark between her and Jack, but she senses there's more to Jack than his easy-going nature. Together, they're in danger of exposing a dark underbelly of lies and deceit running deep beneath the entire community that's far deadlier than fraud.

And whoever is behind those secrets is prepared to kill to keep them quiet . . .

Nowhere

A sadistic killer has come to Long Lakes . . .

After the harrowing events of the past summer, Valentina Bianco is happy to take it easy, working on her wine importing business and enjoying the beauty of her Eastern Tennessee cabin, Elsewhere. With her boyfriend and FBI agent Jack Erikson all the way across the state, working an important case, she's content to have a quiet few weeks ahead of her.

But all is not quiet in idyllic Long Lakes. A new resident has moved into the gated community, a famous actor hiding from his past. He has secrets, and they're about to catch up with him. From the moment he meets Valentina, he develops a keen interest in her, much to the chagrin of a jealous Jack.

When a young woman is brutally murdered, the community's residents are on edge. Who could possibly be behind it? As Valentina is about to learn, everything is not what it seems, and nowhere is safe.